PENGUIN CRIME FICTION

Editor: Julian Symons

WATCHER IN THE SHADOWS

Born in 1900, Geoffrey Household was educated at Clifton and Magdalen College, Oxford, and, on going down, spent four years as a banker in Rumania. Irked by the sedentary dignity of it he set off for Spain to sell bananas, and from there went on to the United States just in time for the Depression. After writing children's plays for radio in the States he returned to England, but shortly afterwards began to travel printers' inks in Europe and South America. Meanwhile *Atlantic Monthly* encouraged him to start writing professionally, on the strength of his short stories. His first novel, *The Third Hour,* was published in 1937 and was followed by a collection of short stories. He was unable to profit by the success of *Rogue Male,* published in 1939, since he had already been dispatched to Rumania as an Intelligence Officer by the time it came out. He remained in the Midde East until 1945 and then had almost to begin again as a writer. Since then he has published several novels, among which are *A Rough Shoot, A Time to Kill, Thing to Love, Olura, The Courtesy of Death, Dance of the Dwarfs, The Three Sentinels, The Lives and Times of Bernardo Brown, Red Anger* and *Hostage: London* (1977); several children's books including *The Exploits of Xenophon, Prisoner of the Indies* and *Escape Into Daylight*; his autobiography, *Against the Wind*; and short stories. Geoffrey Household, who is married and has three children, lives in the country.

GEOFFREY HOUSEHOLD

WATCHER IN THE SHADOWS

PENGUIN BOOKS

in association with Michael Joseph

Penguin Books Ltd, Harmondsworth, Middlesex, England
Penguin Books, 625 Madison Avenue, New York, New York 10022, U.S.A.
Penguin Books Australia Ltd, Ringwood, Victoria, Australia
Penguin Books Canada Ltd, 2801 John Street, Markham, Ontario, Canada L3R 1B4
Penguin Books (N.Z.) Ltd, 182–190 Wairau Road, Auckland 10, New Zealand

—

First published in Great Britain by Michael Joseph 1960
First published in the United States of America by
Little, Brown and Company in association with the
Atlantic Monthly Press 1960
Published in Penguin Books in Great Britain 1963
Reprinted 1971
Published in Penguin Books in the United States of America by
arrangement with Little, Brown and Company in association with
the Atlantic Monthly Press 1977

—

Copyright © Geoffrey Household, 1960
All rights reserved

—

Made and printed in Great Britain
by Hazell Watson & Viney Ltd
Aylesbury, Bucks
Set in Linotype Plantin

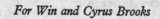

For Win and Cyrus Brooks

I

BURNING BRIGHT

I LOOK back on my course of action as lunacy; and yet at the time it seemed the only way out. Pride, probably. One can never quite escape from one's ancestors. Old Cunobel understood that. But there was a perverted common sense in it, too. The police admitted afterwards that if I had continued to live my normal life – and since I had to work to eat what else could I do? – they would not have been able to protect me.

Ian Parrow saw the position as that of a hunter who is trying to protect some terrified native village from a man-eater. It is no use to cordon the place and post a rifle up every tree. The man-eater simply observes the whole preparation – tempering its disappointment with contempt – and goes away until everyone is sick of the whole business. Then it returns.

In my case there was no one to protect except myself, terrified enough, God knows, for an entire village. But the principle was the same. I had to hunt the poor brute down alone, on foot and on horse, and give him every chance to show himself.

Since the late nineteen-forties I have earned an obscure but very satisfying living as a zoologist, specializing in the life cycles of the smaller European mammals. Experience from youth onwards has fitted me for patient work out of doors in all weather, and I have even learned to enjoy the long hours at my desk, comparing and compiling statistics. English is not my native tongue, but I speak it without accent. As for writing it, the international jargon of scientists generally eases my task. That will not help me here. But I take it I cannot go far wrong if I write as I talk.

On the morning of 20 May 1955, I was working on some weak but fascinating evidence of delayed implantation of the blastocyst in the red squirrel – already proved for the roe deer and the badger – when I heard the double knock of the postman at my front door. It was before eleven and I was alone – thank God! – in the house.

The French windows of my study were wide open. Before leaving the room I closed them to prevent the fresh west wind blowing all the papers off my desk. Then there was a delay of another half minute while the catch of the window gave trouble. Meanwhile the postman, I imagine, was waiting impatiently to deliver his small parcel. When at last I walked up the passage from my study to the front door, its panels disintegrated in front of me.

That was my first impression – through the eyes. Though I was only some fifteen feet away from the door I observed it separating into its original planks before I was conscious of noise and vapour.

The lock had jammed, and there was enough door left, except around the letter box, to obstruct the way out. I ran into the dining-room and out through its now glassless window. On the path lay the upper and lower halves of the postman, joined together – if one could call it joined – by the local effects of the explosion.

The red Post Office van stood at the gate. My very suburban street was filling with people, mostly women. I remember wondering where they all came from. I have a habit of distracting my mind from whatever shocks it by a moment of unrelated speculation. Did those morning houses always hold such an intolerable crowd of untidy human beings behind their closed doors?

The more sensitive stood at my garden gate only for seconds. The rest stayed to stare, gradually infiltrating into the garden. None of them approached the postman. I do not think the reason was the public's callous lack of initiative. It was so obvious that the postman needed no help.

I tore down one of the dining-room curtains with a nervous jerk and covered the body. All the intruders were firing questions at me. I could only reply that I hadn't seen, didn't know, couldn't explain. I vaguely expected some sort of hostile demonstration. Of course there was none. That horrified little crowd assumed that the postman's death was as meaningless as a road accident.

At last a policeman arrived; then, with very creditable speed, a patrol car and a van of police from the borough station. Like a team of well-trained, fatherly sheep-dogs they handled the gaping women, the body and the search for every scrap of paper from the presumed parcel.

I disliked both them and their uniforms. At that time – I think I am over it now – police, even the kindly English police, made me as unreasonably impatient as some ardent pacifist bristling at the approach of a battalion behind its band. I knew of course that it was absurd to resent the obedience of a sheep on an occasion when one could be nothing else and I tried to avoid too aristocratic a coldness in answering their quick, courteous questions. I doubt if I succeeded, but they put my manner down to the effect of shock upon a retiring scientist.

The ambulance came and departed. A policeman was posted on my front gate. I was offered a lift to the station which I accepted, smiling at what seemed to me hypocritical politeness. The detective was hurt. He explained that it really was an offer and that many people were shy at being taken away immediately in a police car when they had witnessed crime or accident; they preferred to make their way to the station independently in order to avoid gossip among the neighbours.

Once in the superintendent's office I was more at ease. The face above the uniform was that of a hard-worked accountant or civil servant. He was a sensible and kindly man of about my own age, and he made it plain at once that he thought me the intended victim of the explosion and in no way responsible for it.

'You know of no motive, Mr Dennim?' he asked. 'No enemies at all?'

I did not. It never occurred to me that anyone could think me worth murdering. But I had been half prepared for some nightmare accusation of blowing up red squirrels and bagging a postman instead.

'Any domestic cause which could help us?'

'You mean a jealous husband or something of that sort?'

'Just any irregularity,' he said quietly in the tone of a father confessor.

'Not on my part. And I am certain you can rule out my aunt.'

'She is unmarried?'

I saw the way his mind was working and suggested that he had better get his own impression of Aunt Georgi.

'She is a widow,' I warned him, 'and of very sane, determined and individual character.'

'Have you any theory of what actually happened, Mr Dennim?'

I had and I gave it to him. When I did not answer the postman's knock, he tried to force the parcel through my letter box instead of leaving it with the next-door neighbours or taking it back for a later delivery. My letter box had a bigger opening than usual; a good-sized book, for example, would fit in. The explosive was probably meant to go off when the string was undone or an interior lid was lifted. But what happened was that the parcel jammed in the box – which might have broken the acid container or released the spring of the trigger device.

I was so absorbed in explanation that I did not see I had given him a clue, harmless enough but inviting questions, to my past life.

'Never blown anyone up yourself, I suppose?' he asked with too forced a heartiness.

'Just an army course on how to do it.'

'You have never had any connexion with – well, any of these violent nationalist groups?'

'No. The parcel could not have been meant for me or my aunt at all.'

'But you said your letter box set it off.'

I told him that it must have been delivered in error, that either the sender got the house number wrong or the postman made a mistake. The street was correct. I picked up and handed over to the police a bit of blood-sodden brown paper which showed the last half of the street name in printed capitals.

'What do you know of your next-door neighbours?'

'We say good morning and comment on the tulips.'

'In your profession as a zoologist you have not come across

anything which could provide a motive for putting you out of the way?'

'I fear my results are not sufficiently spectacular, superintendent. I am only a decided nuisance to one micro-biologist, and even so he moderates his language when I pay him a drink.'

I tried to turn the conversation into the world of science where murder is rare. Presumably rare. After all we have so many ways of making it appear death from natural causes. But the superintendent refused to be side-tracked.

'I gather you were in some branch of Intelligence,' he said. 'Are you sure there is no motive dating from that?'

'I cannot imagine one.'

'Would you care to tell me more?'

I took refuge in the Official Secrets Act and referred him to the War Office. Whatever they chose to tell him – it would certainly be one of those statements of bare facts which look revealing and are not – I knew he would keep to himself. But I was by no means sure that the police did not gossip about any curious stories which they discovered on their own. I did not want my past and former nationality to be known all over the district just because a postman had been killed at my front door. I think I was unjust, but there again my prejudice against police, any police, was at work.

The superintendent got his own back when I left him. I was thoroughly disconcerted by the sight of half a dozen newspapermen in and around the entrance to the station.

'What on earth am I to say to these fellows?' I appealed.

'There is not much I can teach you about keeping back information,' he answered dryly. 'I can only advise you not to make a mystery of yourself.'

In fact it was easy. I played the dull specialist in a dull profession who knew nothing, had noticed nothing and was outraged that there should have been anything out of the ordinary to notice. The representatives of the evening papers were completely taken in. What I said was not quotable either for its inanity or for any intelligent conjecture. Charles Dennim, a zoologist living quietly with his aunt, simply was not news.

Only one of the papers thought me worth a photograph.

Aunt Georgi declared it to be unrecognizable. I looked, she said, like a hangman who had taken to religion. With my face at rest, perhaps it was not very surprising that I should.

Georgina and I shared the house and our small incomes, saving each other from the cheap hotel which might otherwise have ruined our privacy and digestions. It was a natural partnership. We were both survivors from another age – a couple of dinosaurs, let us say – one of an older generation than the other, but both equally successful at persuading a society of little mammals that we were perfectly adjusted to it. As for ourselves, we endured each other in an unbroken state of deep affection and armed neutrality.

Georgina had the genial, positive manners of a trim little cavalry general, retired on a pension. When she wore a bowler hat and riding breeches she could almost pass as one. At the riding school where she was assistant mistress she had been, I understand, occasionally addressed by new pupils as 'Sir'. But never twice.

I met her on her way back from the school to prepare her for the shock of finding no downstairs windows and a policeman at the front gate. She took the news extremely well. It was to her one of those inexplicable happenings in an unreasonably excitable society at which a woman of character shrugs her shoulders. Only the actual absence of windows prevented her saying that the whole affair had been much exaggerated by the Press.

I was therefore surprised when, after dinner, she continued to show a too persistent curiosity. It was not fear. She was quite incapable of nervousness.

After I had made some of the polite but uninterested noises by which one assures a female companion, wife or aunt, that one is listening, she said:

'Charles, you are not to be deliberately stupid! Suppose that package had been meant to kill one of us?'

I laid down the evening paper and remarked that we did not know it was meant to kill anybody.

'Of course we do!'

'We do not. It might have been a packet of detonators which

some damned fool sent through the post. One of our neighbours down the street or next door probably knows what caused the accident and isn't saying.'

'Which next door?'

'I cannot guess.'

'And what was it?'

'Dear Aunt Georgi, how the devil do I know? You have like all women a tendency to argue when there is no evidence to argue from.'

'And you, Charles,' she retorted, 'because the evidence was removed in an ambulance, try to believe that it was never there at all.'

That shot went home. I was so busy suppressing my own horrified disgust that I had also suppressed an uncomfortable whisper at the back of my mind. It had to be recaptured and thought out like the uneasiness which can spoil a morning until one traces it to a dream.

For the next two days nothing happened. Passers-by stared curiously at the house and at the builders who were repairing front door and windows, and continually discovering frames, gutters and plaster which had to be replaced. The superintendent telephoned once for no obvious reason. I continued to question the love life of the red squirrel. Georgina, jodhpured and tweed-coated, strode off every morning to the riding school, her straight back disapproving the vulgarity of crime and its publicity.

Only once did she approach the subject – obliquely, for she would never allow herself to be snubbed twice.

'It may interest you to know, Charles,' she said, 'that there is a new municipal sweeper on this road whose face I do not remember.'

I complimented her on being so observant, and added that there was another plain-clothes cop frequently engaged in changing all four wheels of an old car on the waste ground at the corner of Acacia Avenue.

'They seem to think someone is in need of protection.'

'My own theory, Aunt Georgi, is that they suspect you of posting parcels to me.'

'Pah! Fact is – they don't know any more than we do!'

For the time being she did, I believe, give up any further idea that the parcel was meant for me. So did the superintendent. There were other claimants to the honour of being assassinated. My suburban street was long; still, I should never have guessed that in some three hundred respectable little houses there could be two people who thought themselves important enough to be murdered.

One was a television singer, momentarily resting. She gave the papers an incoherent story of a desperate lover. He really existed. Whenever the psychiatrists pronounced him harmless and returned him to his family, an enterprising publicity agent paid him a small salary. He could be trusted to create a diversion on the doorstep of any female entertainer. But his speciality was threatening suicide. He did not send bombs.

The other was a Cypriot who had a genuinely strong case – though the local police were not sure whether they were Greeks or Turks who thought the world better without him. It was the superintendent who told me all this. He must have had, as I expected, a resounding but reticent report on me from the War Office. He asked me to keep my supposedly experienced eyes open, and accepted my assurance that the parcel could not possibly have been addressed to me. Why shouldn't he? It stood to reason that if I was not confident I would be yammering for protection.

Now that both police and Aunt Georgi had ceased to bother me, my own doubts perversely began to grow. The time of that bomb's delivery pointed straight at me. An assassin who is not normally a criminal must surely take infinite care not to get the wrong man. The Cypriot might have opened his parcel while talking to a friend or his landlady. But if the sender wanted me and only me and if he knew the routine of the house he could be sure that I should be alone in it when the parcel postman called.

This suggested that I had been under close observation and might still be. If I were, some face which was familiar to me on my own street or station ought to turn up again on the Underground or on my usual routes to the London Library, to the Museum, to lunch. When in London I had become very much a creature of habit.

But I could not see a sign that I was followed. That was not surprising if my regular routine had already been checked. For example, it is not necessary for me to disturb an animal by following it about. After a period of patient observation I know what it is likely to be doing and where it is likely to be found at any given time.

I did not change my habits. It was not worth either the trouble or the reproving of myself for undue nervousness. I was still only admitting that it was possible, just faintly possible, that I had been the intended victim of that parcel.

Then there was a curious incident. Not another attempt on me. Nothing but a message, and a very clear one. I received a pamphlet published by some politico-religious society with revolting – and true – photographs of German concentration camps. There was a small cross in one corner of a picture of Buchenwald. It covered the Officers' Mess.

Language is a clumsy way of communication. It takes me thirty-five words to convey the meaning of that cross. Something of this sort:

'You do not appear to be worried. That is a pity. I wish you to be worried. I wish it so much that I do not care if this message sends you to the police.'

The sender could not of course know what I had or had not told the police, but there was no sign that I was being guarded. I must have appeared to him very unimaginative.

All the same it was safe to assume that he would keep clear of my house and street for the next few weeks. The danger, if there really was any, would be outside. I took the precaution of moving about by unusual routes at unexpected times and avoiding the edge of Underground platforms.

Meanwhile I wrote to an old friend in the Ministry of Justice at Vienna. We had lost sight of each other since 1943, but the bond was close. We were both Austrians with a tradition behind us which made us loathe Hitler and every one of his crazed fanatics. I came directly under his orders in the private war which we carried on under instructions from London. The

English are too inclined to think of Germans and Austrians as one people. They forget – if they ever knew – that thousands of us were executed for sabotage.

His reply was immensely cordial. He looked back on that period with enjoyment. Well, perhaps we did enjoy it – for the first year. Death at the hands of the Gestapo had never been, in a sense, more than a day away and we gambled with it. We avoided the thought that if we were caught death would certainly be several months away, and that when it came we should be without nails, teeth, sleep or sanity.

He seemed surprised at my question. He thought the murders would have been reported in British papers. I don't think they ever were. The only foreign murders which interest the British are French.

There have been no known cases of revenge [he wrote] *except upon the former staff of Buchenwald. A certain Gustav Sporn, Major, was shot dead outside his home two days after his release from prison. The assassin left no clue to his identity, and nobody greatly cared. Sporn seems to have been an unspeakable brute, and German opinion (though of course, being what they are, they would never admit it) was that the allies should have hanged him instead of letting him off with a ten-year sentence.*

A month later Captain Walter Dickfuss came out. He was decoyed to a ruined factory where, according to the medical evidence, he was kept alive with great ingenuity for three days. The medico-legal authorities were so shocked by the appearance of his corpse that investigation was and is most thorough.

Obviously the criminal is some poor devil who survived the horrors of Buchenwald. But all possible suspects have been checked. Nothing fits.

The third to go was a fellow called Hans Weber against whom there seems to be nothing at all except that he served in the Gestapo and was a guard at Buchenwald – if one can call that nothing. German police believe that Dickfuss implicated him by some confession, possibly false, during torture.

His was an interesting case, for he was killed in spite of – one might almost say because of – police protection. He was stabbed in a crowd, recovered from a very nasty wound and was then well watched day and night.

The watch began to slack off after a couple of months, as it always does, but the executioner was more patient. All the police know of him – and they are certain of it – is that he must have plenty of money and unlimited time at his disposal.

He pretended to be a cop, frightened Weber out of his life, rushed him round a corner for safety, gave him a drink from his hip-flask. And that was that. The hip-flask is conjecture. The rest is the evidence of Weber's wife. She says that the man was above average height. Otherwise her description of him is worthless. She heard the quick conversation at the front door of the flat but only caught a glimpse of the man's back as he and Weber rushed out. He must have watched the flat until he was sure of the hour when she put the children to bed.

We learned in a hard school not to ask unnecessary questions, old friend, but I am bursting with curiosity. If you are on the trail of the murderer – or shall we call him an executioner? – take it up with Scotland Yard. They will presumably have details of all three cases from Interpol.

There was only one man in whom I felt able to confide. Even him I had avoided for years. I called him up at his farm near Buckingham and asked him to meet me urgently in London at some spot where we could not possibly be seen together. My plan was vaguely forming – clear enough to foresee that there should be no observable connexion between us. He told me that he had the use of a friend's flat and made an appointment for the following day.

Singleton Court was a huge, red-brick block of small flats, built in the middle nineteen-thirties – a regular warren of holes for respectable rabbits without young. As I wandered along the heavily carpeted passages looking for Number 66, I wished we had had something of the sort in central Vienna. Not even a continental concierge could have reported accurately the movements, political tastes, and professions behind such an architect's fever-dream of white-painted, closed front doors. If I had been followed by my enemy – and I reckoned he had experience of how and how not to follow – he could never discover on whom I had called.

The door of 66 opened at once when I rang the bell. At the sight of Ian Parrow I felt a curious mixture of affection and resentment. He carried me back eleven years into a life which had become mercifully unreal to the zoologist. And yet that strained, thin face which smiled in the doorway – a face which used to give the impression of lank, black hair, and office-white skin as marked as a waiter's uniform – had meant to me such personal safety as I could have, and safety, still more important, for my honour and reputation. Its black and white were now muddled by grey hair and sun-tan. The thin mouth which had been too tense for a soldier had relaxed.

And now I must confess my secret. Even today I hate to put it on paper. Yet I suppose every one of us, whatever the nationality, who fought without a uniform or, worse still, in the enemy's, must have memories which defile him and from which he shudders away. Perhaps the aristocratic tradition of my family made it harder for me than most. But the two thousand years of Christianity behind a proud and self-respecting boiler-maker are just as powerful.

My father used to say that the claim of the von Dennims to any Empire of Germans was rather better than that of the Hapsburgs. So it is, if you conveniently ignore – as he did – that our direct descent from the House of Hohenstaufen began with a daughter. However, by 1922 when I was ten, orphaned, and collecting cheese-rinds from other people's garbage cans, the point was of minor importance.

As soon as the inflation which followed the First World War was over and the Austrian Republic securely established, enough was recovered from the utter wreck of the family estate to give me comfort and a good education. I specialized in Forestry and Ecology. Even as a child I was a keen naturalist – too passionately fond of the gun, of course, but that was the fashion of the time.

In 1935 the Government sent me to the United States to study some new forestry techniques and report. I was over there when Hitler marched into Vienna. I did not make any secret of my opinion. Normally that would have been recorded against me; but there were no Nazi spies in the forests of the State of Washington.

Our Canadian colleagues across the border were very friendly, and I used occasionally to meet distinguished visitors from London. It must have been one of those who recommended me as a useful man, but I really do not know through what grape-vine I was tested and recruited.

In 1939 I was cut off by the blockade without a chance of returning to Europe till the end of the war. But I did return. I was flown to London secretly and trained for a year. My chief was Colonel Ian Parrow.

At the end of my training I was returned to the United States – there was no evidence of any sort that I had ever left it – and told how to make my way to Vienna across the Pacific to Vladivostock and on by the Trans-Siberian railway. I managed it, arriving in the spring of 1941 just before Hitler's attack on Russia.

I was not suspect. My story was carefully prepared and unshakeable. I had completed a long and difficult journey to fight for Hitler, and I was held up as an example of the penniless aristocrat who had made good. God, the nonsense I had to talk!

The channel through which I reported and received my orders was that friend, now in the Ministry of Justice, to whom I had written. He had influence and was trusted by the Nazis. He suggested that I was just the fellow to train security units for operation in dense forest. Though the German armies in Russia had complete control of the main routes, they were bothered by the infiltration of agents and partisans. They wanted police patrols which could operate and maintain themselves out in the thick country on the flanks.

I knew more about trees themselves than playing Red Indians, but I quickly became an authority. It was worth the trouble. The continual posting of personnel to and away from the depot gave me a very good picture of troop movements, and I could pass on the information through my cell for transmission to London.

Then I myself was given command of a unit; but instead of sending us to the Russian forests – all armies are alike – we were stationed in the Apennines where a good tree was a rarity.

In Italy there was little I could do beyond letting the organization know I was there. That was a pity, for I had two other patriotic, anti-Nazi Austrians in my command. Our chance came when Italy surrendered. We organized the escape of an entire prisoner-of-war camp – routes, stolen transport, and all.

Owing to long boredom we were careless and came under suspicion. Even so it could only be proved that we had been slack and inefficient. My two collaborators were punished by being drafted to grave-digging, and continued accurate reports of troop movements though they had ceased to move. I, since in a sense I was a policeman, was posted to the Gestapo and soon afterwards sent as an officer to the concentration camp at Buchenwald. It was a studied humiliation of my name. Even Hitler despised the Gestapo.

They may have thought that I would commit suicide. Perhaps I should have done so. Day after day I forced myself to resist the temptation to dig myself in with a machine-gun and kill the swine till I was killed. But Ian Parrow's cold-blooded training counted. I was in charge of records and could read committal orders and abstracts of interrogation. Sometimes the documents showed me what the enemy most wanted to know. It was my duty to get the information out.

Since I was hopelessly out of touch with the Austrian organization, it took me months to reopen some channel of communication. When I did, it was direct to London – usually by secret radio, but surprisingly often by what was practically airmail. Chaos in Germany was beginning, and the night sky was so full of activity that an occasional aircraft could land and take off unnoticed.

As soon as the war was over and the Buchenwald guards arrested, I was spirited away. I was not asked to give evidence at the war trials – partly because I was too valuable to be exposed, partly because Ian understood that I had had enough and that my whole soul was rotted by disgust. It was he who obtained for me British nationality – easily, for there was already a distinguished branch of the Dennims in **England** which had long since dropped the 'von' and the title – **and he** who arranged a future career for me as soon as I had come out of hospital and could bear human society without washing myself continually.

For nine years I had not seen him.

'My dear Charles!' he exclaimed. 'You haven't changed a bit! And what a good little book that was on the squirrel! Obviously they took you for one of themselves!'

He always said in the old days that I reminded him of some confident squirrel flashing a swift look at the intruder before vanishing into the blackness of trees. My russetty colour of hair and skin, I suppose, plus a pointed nose and the angular bones of cheek and jaw. But I cannot see any mischief in my face when I look at it. I am more like a tall, thin, battered monkey than a squirrel.

When we had had a drink together and sung the praises of old friends, I told him the story.

'So it's obvious that someone who was a prisoner in Buchenwald has waited all these years for his revenge. And I am next on his list.'

'But you can't be!' he insisted. 'You weren't a gaoler. You weren't involved in any of the brutality and executions. You were a sort of adjutant, always in the office. Why you? And why now?'

Why me, I could not answer. Why now rather than long ago was pretty plain. Walter Dickfuss had screamed out some accusation during those three days of torture.

'It's more likely,' Ian said, 'that some crazy ex-Nazi who has just been let out of gaol is taking revenge on you for spying on him or Hitler or what-have-you.'

I pointed out that my cover had never been broken. Also I doubted if former enemies ever took revenge on each other when war was long over. It was out of character. They were too tired of it all.

'Yes. I am. Well, we'll go to Scotland Yard straight away. Somebody there ought to remember who I was. You'll be guarded as if you were the Prime Minister.'

'So was Hans Weber,' I said.

'But, damn it, you shall be!'

I reminded him that no private citizen could be efficiently guarded for ever. An assassin ready to wait ten years would be perfectly ready to wait a few months more, taking a look at the set-up from time to time to see how careless the victim and the man in the turned-down hat and mackintosh were getting. I wasn't going to have policemen on my walks, testing my meals, sitting outside the Museum. I hated policemen. I'd had enough of them. And I should be executed just the same – not tomorrow or next week but as soon as we were all convinced that the danger was over.

'Suppose we have your whole story published?' he suggested. 'I should think any Sunday paper would jump at it.'

'I am still not prepared, Ian, to look any person in the eyes who knows I was a captain in the Gestapo at Buchenwald. And what is half the world going to say? The blighter betrayed his country to save his neck, and they gave him British nationality for it.'

'Nonsense! Of course they wouldn't! And what about your Scarlet Pimpernel stuff? There's no trouble in proving that!'

Perhaps. But I then doubted it. It was true that I had planned escapes – could have planned a lot more of them if the wretched inmates of the camp had been lunatics enough to trust a Gestapo captain. The most spectacular was the rescue of Catherine Dessayes and Olga Coronel from Ravensbruck when they were due for the gas chamber. They knew that Hauptmann von Dennim was responsible but they couldn't know that he was not just adding corruption to corruption – a Gestapo swine heavily bribed by the enemy.

'I told you at the time you were a fool not to accept your George Cross,' Ian said.

'One does not defile a decoration.'

'Take 'em a bit seriously, don't you? And anyway it isn't fair to your assassin. It would surely make him think twice if he knew you as Graf Karl von Dennim, G.C.'

'Another very good reason why Charles Dennim should handle him gently and deal with him personally, Ian.'

'Oh, my God, you *would* say that!'

I calmed him down. What I had to propose was really very sensible. I did not want to die in the least – or at least I hadn't wanted to until all these memories were forced back on me – and I did not believe that month after month any police guard could be effective against a man who was patient and implacable, with leisure and money and no criminal record.

But if I could recognize him or describe him, the German police would do the rest. I might even be able to reason with him. At the very worst I could kill him provided self-defence was evident.

'And what I want from you, Ian,' I said, 'is to be my secret agent after all the years I was yours, plus a cottage to live in and an excuse for being in it.'

'A neighbour of mine has got two badger setts on his land,' he replied doubtfully. 'You could be studying their diet. He says they kill his chickens.'

'Well, you can tell him from me they don't. If it isn't a fox – and I suppose he knows – it's probably a polecat gone wild.'

'Jim Melton turned some of his polecat ferrets loose after myxomatosis killed off the rabbits,' he said. 'You could watch the blasted things. Or badgers. The cottage I can manage, though it's some way from my place. But that is all the better. How are you going to persuade him to follow you?'

'By making it easy. As soon as he sees that the house is shut up he can get my forwarding address from half a dozen different places.'

'That will puzzle him,' Ian objected. 'It should be much harder to get your address. If one is going to tie out a fat goat for a tiger, it is essential to let the tiger think he has found it for himself.'

I did not care for the metaphor, though I have since adopted it. But at that first hearing it offended me. It was too typically and heartily English.

'It won't take him long to decide that I am carrying on my normal life and have no police protection,' I said.

Ian thought it most improbable that his tiger would believe

23

me so unimaginative, especially after the pamphlet with the cross on the officers' mess. And if he had me under observation, as he presumably did, he must have seen that I had changed my habits and was offering no easy chances. The right move, Ian suggested, was to appear to have bolted from home in a panic and to leave a trail which could be picked up.

'But what about that admirable aunt of yours?'

'I've fixed that. She'll be staying with a dear old friend of hers who lives near Badminton. All she knows is that I am shortly off on a squirrel-watching expedition.'

'Well, it may work,' he said, showing a first spark of enthusiasm, 'though nothing on earth would persuade *me* to tackle the former Graf von Dennim on ground of his own choosing. All right. First, cottage. Second, a scratch organization to tell you when there is a stranger and what his movements are. But I reserve the right to call in the police when you are certain of your man – and you'll be ninety per cent certain if you see a Buchenwald face which you recognize. Is there anything else?'

'An arm. I have only a sixteen-bore, and that's no good. Nor is a rifle. I must have an automatic.'

'I cannot help there,' he said. 'The police require very good reasons before they will issue a certificate. You'll have to convince them that your life is in danger.'

I impressed it on him again that I was not going to convince the police of anything nor explain to them my past. We argued it all out once more.

At last and rather coldly he declared:

'Very well. I have to admit that this is probably the best way of catching the man. But I can't be mixed up in it beyond a point. Do you realize that if you are caught with a pistol you will be very heavily fined and there will be exhaustive enquiries where you got it from?'

That seemed to me a comically minor risk. Ian had reverted very thoroughly to civilian legality and probably hoped – by God, I could understand it! – that he would never hear of any of his disquieting wartime friends again. Still, he could have used his influence somewhere to obtain an automatic for me. But did he understand, in spite of his goat and man-eater, how close the parallel really was? Perhaps he didn't. He was thinking in terms of a police decoy for catching bag-snatchers in the Park.

That was all. I left Singleton Court – as a matter of principle – by way of the basement and the dustbins, and came out into Gloucester Road. I felt a little more lonely than when I went in – which was most unfair to Ian but may not have been bad for me. Loneliness was a challenge. It shifted my thinking into a gear remembered but long unused.

The question of an arm. To acquire one illegally was a test of how fit I still was to protect myself. I knew no more of criminal society than any other respectable citizen. The fellows who held up bank cashiers must get their weapons somewhere, but the newspapers did not tell us how.

What to wear. A dirty lounge suit, bought cheap and off the peg just after the war, seemed right. A turtle-neck sweater under it was at any rate non-committal. I could not leave the house in them since Georgina's curiosity might be aroused. So I carried the clothes in a brown paper parcel and changed in a public lavatory.

My destination was Soho. After wandering around to find a café where the customers were neither too young nor too exclusively Italian, I entered a revolting joint just off Wardour Street and sat down, speaking just enough broken English to order a cup of coffee. After ten minutes two scruffy individuals, with a show of heartiness towards the foreigner, got into conversation with me and found that I spoke only German. They cleared off soon and sent me a German-speaking lady of the town. She was a hard-faced, rubbery creature of the type to betray her own mother for money. I pretended to be much taken with her and assured her we would have a wonderful time if only I could sell – I swore her to secrecy – if only I could sell a Luger.

The following afternoon I was there again. She introduced me to a large and slimy crook who was an obvious copper's nark. He may have had a police card in his pocket or merely have been in police pay. I don't know. And, to be fair, I suppose he might have been entirely convincing to anyone without a sense of smell trained to spot his type. He was living proof that I was wise to undertake my own protection. If I could smell police, so could my enemy. God knew what the tiger's past had been, but it was safe to assume that he had experience of an underground more deadly than that of London Transport.

My hard-working female friend acted as interpreter. She was disappointed when I denied all knowledge of any Luger. No doubt she had reckoned that a sure couple of quid from the police was a lot better than a mere promise from me.

When the nark had gone she took me to another café where I was inspected from various angles and kitchen doors. There was a good deal of mysterious coming and going – Harry fetching Alf, and Alf knowing where Jim might be and so forth. It struck me that in criminal circles far too many people are expected to keep secrets. At last and in a third café I met the genuine buyer. He could have been anything from a book-maker's runner to a bus conductor. The only quality which one could sense in all that neutral smoothness was contempt for the public.

How was the Luger to be handed over? I put on a show of fear and suspicion, and insisted on a quiet spot where there was no chance of being arrested by the police or set upon by a gang. The rubber lady assisted with a most incompetent trans-lation and made me appear even stupider than the naïve, self-confident type of German crook which I was playing. It was perfectly clear to any person of normal intelligence – and he had plenty – that when he brought the money I intended to hold him up with the Luger and grab it. We arranged a meeting at ten thirty when it would be dark. Cutie was to take me to the rendezvous. He explained to her at length where it was – a bombed site off Haverstock Hill.

I telephoned to Georgina that I should be home late and bought her a box of chocolates of about the right size to hold a Luger. Then I had some dinner and afterwards picked up my cinematically bosomed sweetheart. I was glad to see that she had been instructed to take me discreetly to Haverstock Hill by bus, not by traceable taxi.

She showed me the bombed site and said she would wait for

me. I watched her scuttling off as soon as she believed she was out of sight. It all seemed to be going very well, though I could foresee complications if the buyer brought a companion. I was pretty sure he wouldn't. His own gun – of course I was praying all the time that he had one – should be quite enough to intimidate me.

I waited for him a quarter of an hour, feeling his presence and once hearing him, while he sensibly satisfied himself that I was alone. After that it was all very quick. He held me up straight away and ordered me to drop my parcel. I whined with surprise and terror. It was quite unnecessary for him to tell me what he would do if I raised my voice. He was most disappointed that the likely box contained only chocolates and came for me, as so many men do when they have lost their tempers, carelessly waving his gun about. I had expected it would be more difficult.

But I really did congratulate myself on finesse – until, that is, I examined his automatic. It was a miserable Italian .22, accurate enough for killing but with no stopping power at all. However, it would have to do. I shifted him into the shadow of a wall where he was unlikely to be noticed until he came round, replaced the lid on the box of chocolates and returned to my suburb and my aunt.

2

SPRUNG TRAP

I LOOKED out of the bedroom window of the cottage which Ian had found for me with a rising of spirits that I had not felt for years. Not that the scene was in any way unfamiliar; during many months of field work on the smaller mammals I generally rented a room from some kindly old body who was prepared to make my bed and produce simple meals at irregular intervals. The cause of my temporary content was probably relief at being clear of London.

My vulnerability had been getting on my nerves. There was one duty which I hated: attending as a principal witness the inquest on the postman. Since time and place were public knowledge, my presence was detestably dangerous. It did have one advantage. If my follower was among the public or idly – possibly hopefully – watching from a side street, he could satisfy himself that I was in no way guarded and would feel more free to ask questions.

Both Ian and I felt certain that he would not try to trace me by writing a letter. If I were submitting to the police all letters from unknown correspondents, he would give some clue, however slight, to the postman's murderer for the laboratories to work on.

But he could risk telephoning to Georgina or the Museum or a few other obvious places to ask for my address. None of them had it. I told them all that I had not yet decided exactly where I should be staying and would let them know later. That would look to him as if I had hidden myself or perhaps as if the police had hidden me.

What would he do then? Ask discreet questions. Try the milkman, for example. No luck. The firm of builders repairing the damage? That wouldn't do him any good either. I had made a point of telling the chief clerk that the firm could get in touch with me at any time through the Museum.

What about the plasterer, painter and carpenter working on the house? It was an obvious place for the police to plant an agent. He'd have to be careful with them. Still, if he were patient and prepared to watch the men home he could be pretty sure that they were what they appeared to be. When at last he risked a question, it would give him what he wanted to know. In a great hurry on leaving the house and pretending to be nervous about gutters and the horrid little portico over the front door I had made a disastrous slip and given the carpenter my real address.

It would take time to pick up the clue; but I counted on the care and patience with which he had arranged the execution of Hans Weber. I reckoned that he would spend at least a couple of weeks in finding out the address, arranging a base for himself and avoiding possible traps. Meanwhile I could familiarize myself with the country and watch badgers.

The cottage which Ian had rented for me was in North Buckinghamshire, in the parish of Hernsholt and about a mile from the village. Far away to the north and east stretched the blue-hazed plain of the south Midlands – elm and oak as far as the eye could reach.

It was in fact fairly open pasture neatly and thickly hedged, with only a few small coverts where foxes bred under the clatter of wood pigeons; but seldom were there fifty yards of hedge without a great tree. Seen over distance, as from my bedroom window, England seemed to have returned to the temperate forest out of which the Saxons cut and cultivated their holdings. I felt a deeper sympathy for that solid race of pioneers – because I too was still searching for home – than most native English. They have a romantic passion for the still older strains in their ancestry.

The cottage was known as the Warren. It belonged to a widow who had gone out to stay with a son in Australia, and was still ladylike even when I had packed away all breakable ornaments. It had electricity, a telephone and a water supply piped from a spring at the back.

Around the spring was a copse of willows. It gave little real cover except at night, but I did not care for it until my eyes were accustomed to its light and shadow. In front of the cottage was a half acre of overgrown garden and, beyond it, the Long Down – a stretch of well-drained upland which had been an airfield during the war. The desolate concrete runways, the air raid shelters and the aircraft bays were still there. Over and among them sheep and cattle pastured.

Though it was only fifty miles from London my retreat gave such an impression of quiet remoteness that I began to doubt whether the goat could be found. An address written in a casual workman's notebook seemed a slender connexion with me. Yet it was certain that the tiger would haunt my suburb and finally risk approaching the empty house when every other line of enquiry had failed. When he followed me he should be noticeable. The district was without holiday-makers to confuse the issue. There was nothing to do but farm, breed horses, or fatten cattle.

I spent the first few days completing a fast and thorough reconnaissance of my surroundings. I made no mystery of myself – and the badgers were there in plenty to account for my movements. I decided to have no observable communication with Ian, not even by telephone. His formidable past was too widely known. I wanted to appear friendless and unprotected to any investigator.

We did, however, have an optional rendezvous at a bridge over the slow Claydon Brook on Ian's normal road to and from Buckingham. At four every afternoon he proposed to drive across it. In the stream was a willow snag which he could see from his car. If it had its usual trailer of dead water weed all was well and there was nothing to report. If it was clear of weeds I was waiting close by for an opportunity to talk.

That Wednesday morning, the fifth since my arrival, was a perfection of English early summer. The new leaves of the great pear-shaped trees which closed the horizon hung motionless, awaiting the first trial of heat. After coffee and bacon I idled in the garden, feeling inclined to take a hoe and discourage the weeds like a good tenant instead of doing a third exploration of the Long Down.

The Long Down was important. It would be my main line of communication as soon as there was any suspicious sign of interest in me. I was certainly not going to risk the lane which led to my cottage, bordered by thick hedges on both sides. But moving across the disused airfield I could always be sure that I was not followed; and if I had reason to think I was I could vanish among the aircraft bays and the low brick foundations, overgrown by brambles, where huts had once been. It would be impossible to tell by what path I intended to leave the down or whether I had not already left it.

I decided to weed. I wanted to discourage the dog. It belonged, I was told, to some feckless woman on the far side of the Long Down who worked in a factory at Wolverton and might or might not return home at night. She left the animal outside her cottage with a dirty plate of bread and stale canned dog food. No one would have been surprised if she had expected it to open the cans. The dog spent its days on the down, pouncing disconsolately on beetles, and was delighted to find a companion with nothing obvious and agricultural to do.

I might as well have reconnoitred my territory waving a red flag as followed by this unavoidable dog which had the bounce of a terrier and the reproachful affection of a spaniel, both very evidently among its ancestors. It was not trainable. Even if it had been, no dog – except a poacher's lurcher – can move as silently as a man.

So I spent that gently blazing morning in the garden, and in the afternoon took a bus to Bletchley. I wanted to familiarize myself with the likely routes to and from the station. My very vaguely formed picture of the enemy's character suggested that he might avoid the risk of car number plates, whether true or false, and use the railway. In any case he would soon find out that I avoided roads and that in following my movements between the cottage and the badgers a car was no help. I myself would have liked to borrow one; but I had no car in London – both Georgina and I with our limited incomes preferred wine to petrol – and it might have appeared unnatural suddenly to have private transport at my disposal in the country.

I did my shopping in Bletchley and returned to the cottage

with veal cutlets, new potatoes and peas. Then, feeling the need of human society with which to share my thirst and the beauty of the evening, I strolled up the lane to my village of Hernsholt and entered the Haunch of Mutton.

Ferrin, the landlord, was alone. He was a thin, ironical man in his early fifties with an air of knowing the utter worthlessness of humanity and enjoying it all the same. He was generally smiling and silent, but occasionally produced a comment as devastating as that of some nihilistic cartoonist. The habit was good for trade. Local customers would sit over a second drink in the hope of being shocked by whatever Mr Ferrin might say next.

He served me with a long whisky and soda, and watched me till the glass was nearly empty.

'Like it down here?' he asked.

I said I did, and that it was a peaceful spot.

'Too peaceful for business.'

'They watch the telly instead, I suppose?'

'That won't last long,' he said. 'But they'll soon find something else to stop 'em thinking. It's all up with the pubs and the churches. It wouldn't surprise me to hear of a take-over bid from one or the other any day now.'

I replied that I didn't much care which admirable tradition ran the other so long as it wasn't the popular press. That seemed to please him, but he still returned to probing me.

'My father used to swear there was nothing like a badger ham. You'd be all against that, I expect?'

'Not a bit. But I shouldn't kill in a sett which I was watching. It spoils the fun.'

'Breakfast is breakfast and science is science, like?'

'Exactly.'

'Have another on the house,' he said, refilling my glass without waiting for an answer. 'You should try the bitter some time. It's a small brewery and it don't put water in the beer to pay for the advertising. Colonel Parrow is one of the directors. That's how I come to be here.'

It seemed wise to take advantage of this marvellously oblique approach to my character and my business while we were still alone, though I did not know what story Ian had told him.

'You were under the colonel in the war?' I asked.

'Not under him and not over him, in a manner of speaking. I was mess sergeant in one of his hush-hush joints. And you'd be surprised what I used to hear once they got into the habit of not stopping talking when I came round with the drinks. But if I'd asked a question they'd have hung me from a parachute and dropped me on Hitler. That's what I told Isaac Purvis.'

'Who's he?'

'Works on the roads for the District Council. You said good morning to him the other day when he was clearing a ditch in Satters Bottom.'

'I remember. A little dried-up chap in his sixties.'

'Seventies, more like. Well, day before yesterday a stranger comes up to him and asks which we called the Nash road. Is that of any interest to you?'

I have always been sure that if England were ever occupied its people would find the organization of underground cells an almost effortless means of self-expression. On the surface they are so open, and yet so naturally and unconsciously secretive about anything which is of real importance to them.

'Yes,' I answered. 'But there are four other houses along the Nash road besides my cottage. Was Mr Purvis able to find out which he wanted?'

'No. He couldn't keep him – though he's a rare one for conversation. Lucky if you get away after half an hour of the Council's time! But he noticed the chap didn't go in to Worralls. And I saw Slade and Parrish last night, and he didn't go there. So that only leaves you and Mrs Bunn – who never has a visitor, I'd say, but the vicar and the district nurse.'

'What sort of man was he?'

'Big, dark, clean-shaven.'

'A foreigner?'

'No. A gentleman, Isaac Purvis said.'

On my leisurely way back to the cottage I decided that the enquirer had been someone out for an innocent walk who had asked his way earlier and been told to take the Nash road. It was far too early for the arrival of the tiger.

What kind of man was Isaac Purvis describing? It seemed

odd that one couldn't be both a foreigner and a gentleman. I vaguely understood what he meant from continental parallels, but Aunt Georgina would have been on surer ground.

Any of the younger generation who still used the outdated term at all would probably mean by 'gentleman' a person who was well-spoken and apparently well-educated. But I had a feeling that in the mouth of an old and prejudiced agricultural labourer accustomed to judge from unconscious depths of instinct and experience the word implied the manner and clothes of someone born to the ownership of land. That suggested the phrase of my Austrian friend's letter – man with plenty of money and unlimited time at his disposal.

On the other hand, surely my enemy could not be English? But Isaac Purvis would be unreliable on that point. He was an authority on manner, not on accent and sentence rhythm. It was most improbable that anyone in the district could guess that I myself, for example, was of foreign birth – though a careful listener with some knowledge of other languages might detect it.

All the same, I reminded myself that any doubt was still a doubt and that it might be wise to act as if my cell had passed me a preliminary warning. I avoided the Nash road and the short track which led from it to the Warren. I went home across the fields, passing cautiously through the willow screen to my back door.

The evening sun flooded into the kitchen through the open window. All the sounds were peaceful. Under the window the mongrel from the Long Down was snoring. Above it a bee and two bluebottles were noisily trying to get out in the one place where it was impossible. A chewed mess of brown paper and string was on the floor. The veal cutlets which I had left on the kitchen table were inside that damned dog – as for a moment I called it.

I think I had already opened my mouth to rouse it from its stertorous slumber when I realized that its position under the window, its falling asleep instead of escaping with the loot, its continuing to sleep when I was an angry foot away from it were all wholly unnatural. I backed out through the door, remembering that the executioner of Sporn, Dickfuss, and Weber liked to be in at the death.

The summer silence was still absolute except for the cawing of a rook. I disappeared into the willow copse, keeping the house between myself and the garden, and reached the shelter of the boundary hedge. A deep ditch, taking the water which poured off the Long Down after rain as well as the winter overflow of the spring, bounded three sides of the garden. Very slowly I followed this round to the front gate and back again, inspecting every shrub and patch of cover where a man could crouch and keep the cottage under observation. I had no intention whatever of surprising him, for I had foolishly left the pistol in my suitcase under my bed. I merely wanted to satisfy myself that he was not in the house.

There was nothing to be gained by funking the next step. I had produced the situation I intended to produce. If I cleared out now or ran dithering to the police I should merely have a quite illusory period of peace while the big, dark, clean-shaven gentleman occupied himself with his presumably gentlemanly pursuits and waited.

I took the carving knife from the kitchen and a rolled up rug for a shield. Then I went through those upstairs rooms with all the old technique I could remember – flinging open each door, guarding my back and letting the rug enter first. There was no doubt that on my own ground I was alone.

Having recovered that miserable .22 I sat down in the living-room, first brushing the chair with my hand. I could very well be finished off by the schoolboy trick of a drawing-pin in my seat. But that was carrying imagination a little far. I ordered myself not to overdo precautions. Steady routines would be indispensable and sufficient – like shaking out boots in the tropics before putting them on.

Now what exactly had happened? The first plain fact was that the tiger had decided that speed of action was safer than hanging about and giving a clue to his identity; even if I did have police protection, both they and I were likely to take things easy for the first few days. He must already have got my address through the carpenter. He'd had some stroke of luck there.

I could not believe he had taken the risk of calling at the house.

My return from Bletchley had been observed and my departure for the Haunch of Mutton. Having satisfied himself that the cottage was not watched, he had then walked in and poisoned the cutlets. His next move was doubtful. He might be safely on his way to London, awaiting with interest whatever the papers had to tell him, or he might be still close at hand.

The dog was not yet dead. That had to be explained. If you could not be certain how much time you had to play with, surely you would use a fast poison? Probably he could not lay his hands on one which was quite tasteless. After all he had not the resources of a government or a terrorist gang behind him. He worked cautiously and alone for his own lonely revenge.

I examined the cottage for any conceivable clue to his movements and from old habit looked for a microphone, though I could not imagine what use he could make of it. This led me to the discovery that the telephone had been cut outside the kitchen where it entered the house.

That was a puzzle. Suppose I had discovered the break before I had supper? Suppose there was an arrangement with the police that they were to call at fixed hours and turn up at once if they had no reply? Both those points must have occurred to the man before he cut the telephone. My tentative answer was that the drug did not work instantaneously or imperceptibly. There was half a minute while the victim felt so queer that his one impulse was to telephone a doctor.

The cutting of the telephone. The dog still snoring strongly. Together they answered the question of whether this dedicated executioner had returned to London. He had not. He was waiting close by. He intended – if nobody called and the coast was clear – to finish me off with a knife. And it would be in the character of the man who spent three days on Walter Dickfuss to have arranged that when I awoke I should find him sitting by my side.

I give all this analysis of my thoughts as accurately as I can; but at the time my approach to the problem far more resembled the wordless pictures in an animal brain than the calculations of a computer. I remember balancing the automatic on my palm and chattering at the filament of sunlight reflected on the blue barrel. I remember, too, that my arm was trembling. A lack of recent practice in crawling through ditches may have accounted for that, for I still had not realized what the odds against me were.

Indeed at this point they seemed to be strongly in my favour. I had only to lie up in a position where I could command all entrances to the kitchen in order to disable the brute. Even if the light were too poor for accuracy and I killed him, the dog would be sufficient evidence of self-defence. I was quite confident that I could detect his approach however silent and cautious. His background was certainly formidable, but presumably he had not been trained in forest fighting nor had the ears of a watcher of small mammals.

I was already turning over in my mind possible cover and field of fire when it occurred to me that it was most unlikely he had seen me slipping through the willows and entering the house from the back. In that case, from his point of view, I had not yet come home and eaten my supper.

Then there was nothing for it but to creep out again unnoticed and return plainly and openly by the front gate. It would be far from a pleasant walk. Still, the man could have shot me from ambush any time in the last unsuspecting twenty-four hours and had presumably refrained because he dared not risk attracting police or neighbours. It was unlikely that he would risk it now while the cutlets were waiting.

I put the .22 back in my pocket, slung my binoculars round my neck and entered the willow copse. On the west side of it was a tall oak, strangled by ivy which was thick enough to hold. I scrambled up and perched myself comfortably thirty feet above the ground.

Seen from that height the character of the country changed. The apparent closing in of timber and hedges upon my cottage was a false impression. I was surrounded by miles of grassland divided into fields of five or ten acres – a fact which I knew perfectly well but did not, as it were, feel.

I could be sure that the two angles where the track to the Warren met the Nash road were clear, but I could not see through the hedge on the far side of the road. It would be no place, however, to skulk in hiding and arouse suspicion. The upper windows of the farm they called Worralls overlooked the hedge, and the field beyond it was full of chickens now scuttering and squawking back to their houses for the night.

Wherever the watcher might be, he could never feel secure on that side. The farms were busy and the fields too open. If he had cover to his front he had none behind him. The only place to lie up and observe comings and goings was the Long Down which, close to my cottage and at that angle, did not appear to have any cover at all. Alternatively he could well be up a tree – in which case we were staring at each other like a pair of imitative apes, and seeing nothing.

I climbed down and made my way to Hernsholt across country. So far as the Long Down was concerned, I was in dead ground. From trees on or near the road I used the line of the hedges to protect myself. It was slow going, for I had to squeeze like a rabbit under wire and through thorn. It occurred to me that a horse was the only means of moving fast and decisively over this landscape of meadow, hedge and muddy stream.

When I had reached the back gardens of Hernsholt I cut down into the road and started to stroll home innocently and openly. The light was fading. I tried to persuade myself that there were no holes in my reasoning. With three-quarters of a mile to go to my cottage I realized in horror that there was a large hole. The dark gentleman, wondering if he had somehow missed me, might have made a silent approach to the kitchen window and discovered the drugged dog. In that case he had nothing to lose by waiting for me in the dusk alongside the road and taking a close-range shot from either of the hedges.

Never before had I known the madness of fear. During the war I had been afraid – sometimes reasonably, sometimes beyond reason – of arrest and execution, but I felt part of a team who were all enduring the same risk and uncertainty. I was sure of my technique. And, though I seldom saw a confederate, I was not alone.

In this simple walk along a deserted, darkening road there was none of the high morale which comes from outwitting the enemy. Defence was so limited. I could not shoot first. I might bag the wrong man. Even if I got the right one, it could be most difficult to prove his intentions to the satisfaction of a jury, for he sounded like a man who would be above suspicion. It was quite possible that his identity could not be established at all unless he were caught on the body of his victim. The parallel with a man-eating tiger was uncomfortably close.

The sun had set, and light was patchy. The leaves of the eastern hedge reflected the red of clouds and emphasized every block of darkness. Under the shadow of the western hedge both solid and space were dark grey. What appalled me was that there was no safety in vision. My eyes were continually attracted by the light in the west, and what was ahead of me appeared the darker. As for my ears – I once heard the click of a safety catch, dived headlong into the ditch and stayed there until I heard it again. It was a damned starling clicking its beak.

I reminded myself again and again why I was taking this risk. Because I had to go home and turn the lights on. Because then, after giving me a chance to eat the poisoned meal, the enemy would come in expecting to find my body on the floor. Because I wanted to live my life without fear of assassination and no police could ensure it.

All woulds. All mights. It was futile to try and guess what this sort of animal would do or where it was. Its only predictable qualities were patience and ferocity. And meanwhile the 'is', the here-and-now, was a panic of hedge and shadow, of colours like dried blood and arterial blood.

Once I ran and checked myself with an effort. Once I saw a broken oak twig pointing straight at me, half drew the pistol, saw it was hopeless and put up my hands. That was the end. I swore at myself under the name of Graf Karl von Dennim. What the devil would my father have thought of me?

I found such pride surprisingly calming. This conjuring up of an imperial and famous family, which I had never taken seriously since 1918, seemed to make sense of what Charles Dennim, zoologist, was doing. Having accepted British nationality, he owed his feudal service to the Crown. He was at the moment – besides his personal interest in the matter – engaged in avenging the death of a very humble servant of the Crown: a postman.

This preposterous romancing, this sudden, unexpected result of the conditioning of a child who was a gallant little fellow up to the age of six, made me pay more intelligent attention to the road of shadows. It would have been pleasanter to render feudal service with a drawn sword and few well-moustachioed retainers than to walk through grey-green darkness – the red was now low in the sky – with a toy gun which had to be kept half hidden until it was too late to draw it. But at least I could now listen to the regularity of my own lonely steps padding along the road.

I turned at last into the track which led to the Warren and opened the front door. The .22 was in my hand now, and if he had been waiting for me he would have died first. Without turning on the lights I searched all the rooms, coming last to the kitchen. The snoring had stopped. The dog had been removed. All that remained was the torn, chewed paper on the floor together with other evidence, carefully left in place under the window, that a dog had been about. The telephone wire had been inconspicuously repaired.

What had happened was clear. My first home-coming and stealthy departure had not been observed – for the man would never have come back to remove the dog if he knew that my suspicions had been aroused but did not know where I was. I could have gone to fetch the police. To take such a risk was not in his character.

No. He had waited and waited for my return, crept up close to the cottage when the light began to fade, and then to his astonishment heard the snoring. He entered boldly and found – only a dog.

So much for panic! He may never even have thought of ambushing me on my way back, for there was no telling when I would be home. I might have decided to watch badgers. I might have gone off with some casual acquaintance. And meanwhile he had to consider his own timetable and line of retreat.

I was confident that he had gone. Still, it would have been rash to turn on the lights or to eat anything which could be quickly and easily contaminated. Vanishing into the willow copse with an unopened tin of corned beef, blankets and a ground sheet, I slept alongside a fallen branch. Soundly, too. Experience counts. No one on a moonless night can distinguish a man rolled in a dark blanket from a log.

In the damp, sweetly scented dawn I lay there thinking it all out. The Long Down – that, of course, was where he had been hiding, with a perfect view of the track, the gate and the front door. He had no reason to spend an uncomfortable night there. He would sleep in London or wherever he was staying and return in the morning. Why shouldn't he? Nothing was known against him. He could say good morning to me or to a police-man with every appearance of a clear conscience.

I breakfasted on the inside of the loaf – with some hesitation, but I was too hungry to fuss – and cleaned up the cottage and myself. At nine the telephone rang. I let it ring while I did some quick thinking – for there was nobody in the world who could be calling me except Ian and my enemy. Taking cover round the corner of the kitchen, I knocked the receiver off with a long-handled feather brush. Nothing blew up, so I answered. At the other end, to my utter amazement, was Aunt Georgina.

'But how in the world, dear aunt, did you know I was here?' I asked.

'And if you knew you were going to be there, my dear nephew,' she retorted, 'why the devil didn't you give me your address?'

I could tell from her voice that she had hitched up her skirt – as a man hitches his trousers before exercise – and was settling down for a long chat. It was soon plain how the dark follower had picked up my scent.

'After you dropped me at Paddington Station,' she said, 'I suddenly remembered I ought to have packed my boots and breeches.'

I remarked that she always looked very well in jodhpurs.

'But they might have wanted me to show Nur Jehan. And I couldn't know that they weren't all terribly smart and county.

So I wired the admiral that I would take a later train and went home to get a proper outfit. Then someone from the Museum called up to ask for your address. Didn't catch his name. Dr Paffletrout it sounded like. But your colleagues do have the most extraordinary names, Charles.'

This engaged her for some while. She always found the names of international science a matter for robust comedy. When she returned to the point, it was to say that she had told Dr Pizzlefish that she hadn't got my address, that I was travelling and would let her know it later. The carpenter, passing the telephone, had then offered the information which I had privately given him before Georgina and I left the house. There it was. Simple as all that.

Under what observation our devoted sentry kept us I do not know. It must have been close unless he had the luck to see us drive off in a taxi while he was carrying out a routine patrol. I suspect that he then followed us to Paddington, lost touch with me when I jumped on a bus to catch my train at Euston, and trailed Georgina instead. As soon as he saw her return to the house he dashed straight for the nearest telephone box on the off chance that he might get my address.

And now I must go back to explain the boots and breeches at the risk of resembling my dear aunt whose conversation, like that of many intelligent women, only made sense retrospectively. I mean that it appeared incoherent until it arrived at its destination – when all the rest, if you could still remember it, fell into place and was relevant.

Two days after the death of the postman had been reported in the papers an Admiral Cunobel called at the house. He ceremoniously presented himself and his card, and regretted that Georgina was out. He had known both her and my parents in old days.

I asked him in and gave him a drink. I had not then received the pamphlet on which the Buchenwald officers' mess was marked with a cross, and I was sure – almost – that the bomb could not have been meant for me. So I had no reason to be cautious with strangers.

I suspected that he might have something to do with the

police. But it was not that at all. He was genuinely anxious about Georgina. He had lost track of her completely until he read of the zoologist and his aunt who taught riding. He had guessed – though he didn't say so – that our simple life might be seriously disturbed by any emergency, and I think it had shocked him.

He was an arbitrary old charmer whom long years at sea had preserved from most modern thinking which was not professional. As he perched himself on the edge of my desk with a tumbler of pink gin beside him, he resembled a young tortoise eagerly exploring a new lettuce bed. The beak, the jowls and the leathery skin were unmistakable tortoise, but the sprightliness of pale blue eyes and dark blue suit suggested that he still enjoyed himself.

'As a matter of fact, we have met before,' he said.

'I ought to remember, but . . .'

'No, you oughtn't! You were two weeks old! In 1912 I was Assistant Naval Attaché in Vienna, and your mother was extraordinarily kind to me. Those were the days, my lad! None of this nationalism except among the lower classes! A man chose the side he would play for like a county cricketer. County of birth or county of residence – whichever he pleased, but he had to stick to it. I knew your Uncle Willie who fought for the Tsar in the Imperial Guards and your Uncle Fritz who called himself a Bavarian and was killed before Verdun. And Hildegard who married a Greek and nearly got shot by both sides for helping prisoners to escape. And your dear Aunt Georgina who, I don't mind telling you, would have married me if she hadn't fallen in love with her second cousin, the English Dennim. What a horseman he was! Delightful boy, too! Good Lord, he'd be seventy-three now if he hadn't died of wounds on the Somme!'

He went on and on, and I mentioned my surprise that he could remember all the ramifications of my family.

'Had to, my boy! Came under the head of useful information in those days. If you weren't in the stud book yourself, the next best thing was to know who was. I remember fretting about it with your mother. It's all tradition, she said, and none of us

43

can prove more than half of it. I'll fix you up, she said –
Cunobel from Cunobelinus. Shakespeare's Cymbeline. Oldest
pedigree in Europe, if only you could fit a few missing pieces
into the puzzle. And damned if she didn't get Georgina to
spread the rumour! God bless my soul, the Cunobels are a
sound Cornish family, but small, small! But it was just like
your parents. Anyone they befriended had got to have everything they could give.'

I liked him very much, and we went out to lunch at his club.
There, after doing me very well, he ventured on to the subject
of Georgina and the bomb. It must have been a shock. Had
she anywhere to go for a holiday? He owed the Dennims the
happiest two years of his life. Did I think he might pick up old
friendship?

I said that I was sure he might, but that Georgina could be
very difficult if she suspected that anything was being arranged
for her behind her back. She was extremely proud of her inde-
pendence and did not care if she gave the impression of a hard
woman. That made her easy to live with. She neither permitted
her privacy to be invaded nor intruded upon that of anyone
else.

The admiral explained that he was a bachelor – which of
course made it unthinkable that Georgina should stay under
his roof. I did not dare to smile. And in a way he was right.
In spite of the fact that she was over sixty and he well over
seventy, their vitality was such that any healthy and normal
village would at once create a joyous legend about them.

No, what he had in mind was that she should stay as his
guest, but with the vicar – where she would be doing him a
great favour as well.

'The man's in a mess,' he said. 'He could do with some
help.'

I indicated that Georgina's general air and outspokenness
might be disconcerting to a strange vicar.

'Blood and bones, boy, I didn't mean sewing his surplices!'
the admiral exclaimed. 'He's taken to horse-breeding!'

'With an eye on the 2.30?'

'No, no, no! A crazy parishioner left him his pet Arab stallion.

44

Keeps it in the Glebe meadow! Not even properly fenced! Too long a story – but the poor fellow is spending all his money on oats, and he and his daughter have to live on porridge. Well, Georgi might make some sense out of it. I'm bothered sick about the vicar, and I can't keep an eye on everything which goes on in the village any longer.'

When I reported to Georgina in the evening that Admiral Cunobel had called on her and taken me out to lunch instead, I detected a sudden aura and fragrance of femininity. How, I don't know. She neither fluttered nor giggled. I suspect that she immediately saw herself in a ball dress of 1912 and projected the image. She had been a very beautiful girl.

She invited the admiral to tea. This was a ceremony. Her friends and mine occasionally took a meal with us, but we had no pretensions; they ate whatever there was and drank a glass or two of wine as a symbol of hospitality. About twice a year, however, Georgi formally invited somebody to tea. She polished the silver tea service, made a number of tiny cakes and two big ones, cut paper-thin bread and butter in white and brown, and prepared every single offering proper to the tea cult of the older landed gentry. The illusion was complete. The parlour-maid in dainty cap and apron so obviously brought in the silver tray and the muffins that it was an effort to remember one had not actually seen her.

By the afternoon of the tea party I had received the letter from my Austrian friend and knew what I was in for. I was most anxious to get clear of London and have room to defend myself. I was determined that the admiral's invitation should be accepted, for I could not leave Georgina alone in the house. Quite apart from unknown risks, tarpaulins, dust and scaffolding were depressing. The minor damage done by the bomb had revealed that the Victorian woodwork of the house-front was rotten and ought to be replaced.

Peregrine Cunobel's tactful command was perfect. I could see how he had become an admiral. When the conversation had drifted away from 1912 he soon had it firmly anchored to country life and the church.

'If the parsons can't get a living wage,' he said, 'they have to do what they can – grow flowers for the market or turn the vicarage into a guest-house. Mine thinks he can breed horses.'

And then he gave us an enchanting picture of the young stallion, Nur Jehan, which aroused Georgina's curiosity and challenged it. She had gentled horses which had been stupidly or cruelly broken, but had never attempted to discipline a horse which had been brought up as a pet.

When I added that I myself had long been wanting to study a whole colony of squirrels of which I had heard, she agreed that the house would be lonely. And that was that. She accepted Cunobel's invitation to Chipping Marton.

It was from the vicarage that she was telephoning. She hoped I would come over for the week-end and stay on indefinitely if I wasn't bored. Dear Peregrine had already written to me. I gathered from the adjective that she was enjoying herself.

Her pungent chronicle of the doings of the vicar and Nur Jehan made good listening, but I found it difficult to remain patient while keeping an eye on the two windows which commanded the telephone. She did not return to the question of why I had not given her my address – which was typical – and repeatedly wanted to know if I was all right and comfortable, which was not typical at all. I managed to avoid a definite reply to the invitation. I hoped that by the week-end I should be a free man, and have given the police the name and description of the postman's murderer.

I felt quite certain that he would not lose all the advantages he had gained by speed. He had only failed to get me owing to the unforeseeable accident of the dog, and he could not be aware that he had aroused any suspicion whatever.

What had started as Ian's crude goat and tiger was now beginning to have more resemblance to the German Intelligence chess, in which a player never sees his opponent's men at all. He is told by a referee when a move is impossible and when he has taken or lost a piece. From that he must construct his own picture of the squares which are occupied and the pattern occupying them.

What was the enemy's picture? That the police might have

advised me to go into hiding, but that they were giving me as yet little or no protection on the ground. In that case the more he delayed, the more risk he was running. Today, Thursday, by nightfall he ought to be miles away from Hernsholt, unsuspected and satisfied that I was dead.

What was my picture? That he was so close on top of me that I must play for getting a look at his face without provoking an attack or alarming him. The latter was most important. I did not want him to break contact and wait weeks or months for an easier chance.

If he were on the Long Down watching the front of the house it should be possible to see him from the upstairs windows. Presumably he was well aware of that and did not dare to scratch himself or blow a fly off his nose unless he knew where I was.

So I let him know. I took out a deck chair through the front door, went back again for a book, a table and a pile of manuscript, and settled down under cover of the shrubbery – apparently to work. I then returned to the house on my stomach by way of the ditch and the back door.

Hidden behind the bedroom curtains I searched the Long Down with my glasses. There wasn't a sign of him. I gave him up. Perhaps I had exaggerated his energy; perhaps he had decided to be as slow and careful as in London. I took to watching a hare which was hopping along the skyline two hundred yards away.

Now, a hare only sees at the last moment what is in front of him; he can see with very little effort what is behind. So when he jinked and galloped off at an angle to his feeding course I knew the exact spot where something had frightened him. Through the glasses I picked up a shadowy black thread behind the waving grass. It was the top of the entrance to an old air-raid shelter.

I had missed it in my own explorations of the Long Down because I was mainly interested in routes. There was no urgent need to map out the points from which an attack might be made. In any case the shelter was not at all obvious. It had been sunk deep into the clay, and the curve of the roof did not show above ground. Possibly it was meant for the special security VIPs arriving at the airfield.

Whether my own particular VIP was in it at the moment I could not be sure. Standing on the steps of the shelter with his eyes at ground level he could look out with little chance of being spotted by me or anyone else. It was fortunate that he did not want to be seen carrying a rifle about. Or perhaps he felt that a shot at two hundred yards was too much of a gamble.

After a while I detected movement which suggested the top of a head. I could have stalked him from behind, but I had not a scrap of evidence against him. The person in the shelter might have been a retired bishop writing a monograph on the reproduction cycle of the hare. So I wondered if he would take an opportunity to show his intentions. I worked my way back to the shrubbery and returned openly to the house with my deck chair and papers.

Fussing with note-books and binoculars and making a show of an innocent naturalist off for a walk, I set out by the front gate, rounded the garden and skirted the edge of the Long Down close to his shelter. I was aiming for a lane running straight to the west for a quarter of a mile which would allow me to see if I were followed. By the time I was approaching the end of the straight there were two men behind me and a woman on a bicycle. One of the men was a biggish fellow and coming along at a good pace. I hoped he was the right one.

The lane brought me on to the main Aylesbury road, along which I walked for half a mile. He was still behind me, but that proved nothing. I took a turning to the right leading gently uphill to the village of Stoke. If he, too, came to Stoke it would be a strong indication that he was following me, for the route was roundabout. Whoever he was, he had come from the Long Down and the shortest way from there to Stoke was through Hernsholt.

A quick glance through the leaves of the hedgerow showed him two curves behind and coming up fast. So, on reaching Stoke, I hesitated outside the church to admire one of those squat, square towers which make the English landscape but have no other aesthetic value, and then went inside. I hoped that he would also pretend an interest in ecclesiastical architecture and that I should have a chance for a good look at him. But he was content to wait.

On my way out I stopped to chat with the first person I saw, so that I could walk through the churchyard keeping my eyes open but apparently deep in conversation. He turned out to be the gravedigger and by no means a merry one. He informed me that in the midst of life we are in death and that they ought to 'ave cremation wherever the blue clay wasn't no more than four feet down. Press a button, like. By the time I had recovered from the superstitions of an Austrian nursery the feet which had padded after me were strolling away from the church.

I had not thought out what was going to happen now or where I should go. Obviously he could not trail me indefinitely through a network of lanes. If he came close enough to see what turnings I took he would arouse suspicion. If I let him follow me without noticing him, so should I.

The best game for the moment seemed to be to lose him. What would he do then? Return to the Long Down presumably, or perhaps visit the cottage in my absence and attend again to the larder. In either case he would take the shortest way and, if I could get ahead of him, I should at least be able to see his face.

Thought of the larder reminded me that I was very hungry. I bought some biscuits in the village shop. When I came out he was at the other end of the street, looking at a rack of picture postcards hung up in the entrance to the Post Office.

As I started to walk in his direction he went on ahead, taking the road I expected. He may have intended that I should pass him. Once clear of Stoke, the road ran between high hedges and was little used, especially at lunchtime. He would not have dared to allow himself time for any luxurious revenge, but a quick killing and a get-away across the fields was easy.

Now at last my choice of open country was paying off. I vanished into the courtyard of a pub, passed through it and through the kitchen garden into a field beyond. There, under cover of a haystack, I took a quick look at the inch Ordnance

Map. As I thought, there were no obstacles and the contours favoured me. If I hurried I could get ahead of him.

I was out of breath and bleeding from barbed wire and haw-thorn when I reached the road from Stoke to Hernsholt. I found as good a place as his own on the Long Down. I could watch him coming along the road until he reached a bend, and I could then slither down to the hedge and see him pass me on the other side of it at a distance of two or three yards.

I ate my biscuits in peace, for he took a long time to arrive. He may have guessed that I had gone into the pub and waited for me to come out. At last I saw him, the pair of us separated only by a thin screen of wych elm.

The man who passed me was utterly unlike my mental picture of him. He could have taken a room opposite my house and never been suspected. Dressed as a high civil servant with umbrella and brief-case he might have passed with a nod through any police cordon which was guarding me. Isaac Purvis's description of him as a gentleman was right. He be-longed to what it is the fashion to call the Establishment – though I have never had a satisfactory definition of what the devil, if anything, the Establishment means.

His age was close to my own, between forty and forty-five. He wore a brown tweed suit of excellent cloth and a lighter brown cap. His hair – so far as I could see it – was dark, and greying at the temples. He was a heavy man, six feet tall and weighing all of thirteen stone, but moving lightly with a hint of well-trained muscles. For the minor details – his nose was strong and regular, his eyes brown, and he had marked, untidy black eyebrows.

I was sure I had never seen him before. I couldn't have for-gotten such a man, however emaciated, if he had been a prisoner in Buchenwald. And his nationality was, on the face of it, obviously British. But he might not be. I couldn't say why. Manner when alone, perhaps. I wanted a little more eccen-tricity from him. An Englishman of that class plays with his thoughts when he is alone and only looks formal if there is someone to see him.

On the other hand, he had no variety of thoughts to play with. He had only one. I never saw such a set and concentrated expression; he might have been tracking me one single bend of the road behind me. And the spring when he caught up would be as deadly as any tiger's – merciless, for that man believed he was executing those whom the law had not considered quite worthy of death. Yet a general motive was not enough to account for such patience and dedication. There must surely be a precise and personal motive. What was it? I expected to know as soon as I saw him, but I still did not.

It was now that a plan occurred to me, partly because I was close to one of the badger setts which were my cover for staying in the district, partly because I was most reluctant to spend another night at the Warren.

My intention was to trap him unhurt – or only slightly hurt. The case against him for the murder of the postman was building up. He must have been seen in my suburb; and here he was again on my tail. Looking at it, however, from a weary inspector's point of view, there was still no evidence but the word of an ex-Gestapo officer who very deservedly saw things under his bed, and could give no clear and sane motive for being persecuted by someone who was not in Buchenwald – or indeed by anyone who was.

If this fellow was of irreproachable character and standing – which was the impression he gave me – he could not be arrested, only questioned and then carefully watched while his description was circulated to German police. That was not good enough. That would not put him out of action and give me freedom from fear.

Clear evidence. A charge upon which he could be held in gaol while full investigation of him was made. Those were what I must have. And if he would kindly look back once more to see if I were coming along the road behind him, I thought I could get them.

I gave him three minutes, then climbed a gate into the road and followed. I felt pretty safe. There was no reason for him to hang about or double back. What he ought to do before giving me up altogether was to sit down in comfort by a line of firs above and to the right of the road. From there he could probably see Stoke and certainly see me, strolling innocently along right into that shot from the hedge which I had so dreaded the night before.

I did not oblige him by going all the way, but turned off to the left along a fieldpath. The country was open. If he were up among the firs he could see all my movements through his glasses – a most expensive pair which I envied – until I arrived at the patchy cover where the badger sett was.

It was a typical badger fortress, under a tangled mass of thorn and blackberry about twenty yards long, which ran at right angles to a muddy stream. If I had really been intending to study the two or three families which lived in it – there were too many runways for easy observation – I should have crossed the stream and squatted wetly among the rushes to watch them drink and possibly play. But that was an impossible place to tie out the goat for the tiger.

At the other end of this thick wall of vegetation, and a few feet away from it, was a solitary, stunted alder. I cut and twisted a few branches to form a seat in the tree. To make it perfectly clear what I was doing I sat in it and tested it. I also took out my note-book and jotted down details of badger paths and scratching trees. All the time I was careful to remain in sight of the firs on the higher ground.

But my guess that he was there proved wrong. My guess that he was watching me was right. That was typical of all our moves, his as well as mine. There were too many 'ifs', and each of us was inclined to mistake a queen for a pawn.

While I was working on the alder, something disturbed the birds upstream where the banks were over-grown. I paid no attention. A couple of minutes later I went round to the other side of the badger fortress, found a place where the vegetation was thin and searched the stream with my glasses. He was there all right, and he had not come down from the firs or I would have seen him. He must have been waiting for me where the road crossed the stream – an admirable place for the temporary disposal of a body. When I turned off into the footpath I had been dangerously close.

So long as he saw me, I did not care where he saw me from. I hoped that all this preparation of the tree would not puzzle him. He looked the sort of person who would recognize a badger sett – he could take it for a fox's earth if he liked – and would realize that I meant to watch whatever was there from the alder after sunset. It was wildly improbable that he would suspect the truth: that the alder was futile for observation and that I had chosen it because I could be stalked with such ease up the blind side of the fortress.

At last I walked away downstream, leaving him to examine at leisure what I had been up to. When I was out of his sight I broke into a trot, for I had only half an hour to reach the rendezvous with Ian, whose help was essential.

I reached the bridge in time and was just about to go down to the willow snag and clear away the tail of dead water weed undulating in the slow current when I saw old Isaac Purvis leisurely scything the young nettles on the green verge of the road. His bicycle leaned against the hedge – a marvel how the old boy could cycle for miles with the scythe wrapped in sacking over his shoulder – and he appeared to have started on a job which the Rural District Council could well have left till July.

He leaned on his scythe when he saw me hesitate at the bridge, his whole attitude an invitation to join him and talk.

'Nettles are coming on fast this year, Mr Purvis,' I remarked.

'Grass is what I were cutting,' the old man answered, 'a goodish step back, t'other side of the bridge.'

He waited with mischievous eyes to be asked why he had moved. So I did ask.

'You go on up the road, Purvis, says Colonel Parrow, and if you sees the perfesser you give 'im this 'ere!'

He slid into my hand a sheet torn from a note-book as neatly as if he were passing a betting slip under the eye of a policeman.

I have a feeling you may want to see me today. I shall be at the bridge about half past four. There's another report of the stranger whom Ferrin mentioned to you, and I am trying to account for him.

'Very kind of you, Mr Purvis,' I said.

'It was them Boers what started it,' he remarked obscurely. 'Never 'eard of 'em again we wouldn't, if 'tweren't for the Kaiser and 'Itler.'

I had to think that one out. There was a sort of mad logic in it, for British insolence and weakness in the Boer War – or so I believe myself – were both partly responsible for 1914.

'You fought in South Africa?' I asked.

'Ah. Yeomanry. And me bowels never been the same since.'

I agreed that the campaign must have been frightening.

'Went down with enteric, I did, like all me troop. And I'll tell you what cured me though you won't 'ardly believe it. I was ridin' along scarcely 'oldin' on me 'orse when one of them bloody Boers ups and shoots me through the guts. And when I gets to 'ospital I 'ear the doctor say: well, we ain't got to bother about perforation now, 'e says, because 'e's perforated. I didn't rightly know what 'e meant, but I says Hallelujah for me luck and I gets well. So when Colonel says to me: it's a question of atomy, Purvis, I says: well, they won't get un, Colonel, not them Boers nor the Americans neither.'

It looked as if Ian had thought that a zoologist was insufficiently melodramatic for his village. If atomy was what I supposed – it seemed an excellent word – I was evidently a professor with some unspecified interest in nuclear fission.

'What did you think of this big, dark man who wanted to know which was the Nash road?' I asked as soon as I could get a word in.

'A pleasant-spoken gentleman,' said Isaac Purvis, as if that was about as far as he could safely go. 'Put me in mind of old Worrall, 'e did.'

'How do you mean exactly?'

'Old Worrall who 'ad the farm opposite where you're a-staying. I used to work for 'im as carter thirty year ago, and I can see 'im as plain as I sees you. Just as pleasant as ever, 'e was, after 'is eldest son 'ad been took to the mad 'ouse, and you'd 'ave reckoned 'e thought nothing of it. But one day 'e says to me: God Almighty is goin' to pay me for that, Isaac.'

'And what happened?'

'Nothing. What *was* there to 'appen? 'Is eyes were what I meant. Like a widder's eyes when the parson tells 'er that sufferin' is good for 'er.'

That vivid phrase brought back my unreasonable sense of guilt, which had been dispersed by fear and anger. Poor devil – if he believed I was the same sort of creature as Sporn and Dickfuss he had a right to kill me. How long is it since revenge was considered a virtue in a man of honour? A mere three hundred years?

I asked Purvis if he had any reason to think that the big, dark man was a foreigner.

'Well, all I've seen of 'im was three days back. I tells 'im what 'e wants to know. And when I asks 'im if 'e weren't the new undertaker what Mrs Bunn wishes to make 'er own bargain with, 'e just says that 'e weren't.

'I knew as 'e weren't. 'E was just out for a walk in a manner of speakin'. But I says to myself afterwards, I says, now if 'e was the kind of gentleman what ain't in a 'urry and goes walkin' when 'e could do it easier in 'is motor car, then 'e'd like to 'ear about Mrs Bunn making 'er own arrangements with the undertaker. So I wouldn't say 'e ain't a foreigner and I wouldn't say 'e is.'

Mr Purvis was willing to discuss till five o'clock the character of Englishmen – by which he meant the inhabitants of Buckinghamshire and Northamptonshire. That was perhaps a long time to stand chatting in the open when I did not know where our gentleman had gone, but I did not wish to offend so useful an assistant by cutting him short.

At half past four Ian arrived. We drove off in his car. He seemed a little cold and military because he could not find a certain Jim Melton for whom he had been looking. The only time you could be sure of seeing the blasted man, I gathered, was when he was going into the Magistrates' Court to pay a fine for some minor offence or coming out again; and then if you didn't catch him on the court steps he vanished. An enviable gift, I thought.

Ian wanted me to go with him to Buckingham and have a leisurely dinner somewhere afterwards. When I told him to park the car by the roadside and settle down with me under a convenient haystack, he said he could not see why I found boy-scouting necessary. It was an effort to remember that he knew nothing of the last agitated twenty hours.

I gave him my story from the time I had left the Haunch of Mutton the night before. He did not interrupt. He was always a patient and practised listener, though one never knew what explosion there might be at the end.

'But you'd got him cold!' he exclaimed. 'Why on earth didn't you hold him up in his bunker or on the road?'

I reminded him that I dared not shoot. There was no evidence to connect this harmless stroller in the brown tweed suit with the dog or with any attempt on me. I might have a fearful time clearing myself if I killed him. And one of us would almost certainly be killed. The fellow was capable of being just as dangerous as any wounded tiger. Even if I could drill him through the shoulder or shoot his gun out of his hand – and I was too long out of practice to be sure of either – my .22 wouldn't stop him.

'You must have full police protection at once,' Ian insisted. 'Don't you care whether you're alive or not?'

'Very much. I have a lot of work still to do on the red squirrel.'

I am told that was what I answered. It seems unlikely but possible. At that time I felt that my executioner had a good deal of perverted right on his side. The same memories which obsessed him were, after ten years, still present in my own mind too. So I was not then in love with life for its own sake. Being a healthy animal I was afraid of death. Indeed I was never far from the edge of panic. That can be taken for granted; I needn't describe it over again. But I found it hard to give a good reason – beyond the red squirrel – why I should live.

I asked him to forget the police for the moment. What I needed was a witness, preferably him. And then I drew him the sketch map which I reproduce here:

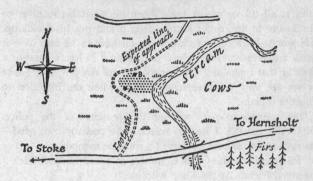

'The trap is timed for the very last of the light,' I explained. 'That is when he will come, for he can't see to shoot later. Here is the layout:

'I am sitting in the alder at A, pretending to watch badgers. He will not take the footpath from the Stoke–Hernsholt road because I could see him as soon as he could see me. He is assuming that I feel well hidden in this bit of country and pretty safe – but I should not be feeling so safe that I would allow an unknown person to approach me after dark.

'He won't come across the stream because the banks are boggy and he would make a lot of noise. So he will come down the footpath from the north. He has soft turf under foot, and he is hidden from the alder all the way. So he has only to put his hand round the edge of that patch of thick stuff where the badger sett is in order to drop me out of my tree with absolute certainty at a range of five yards. If no one pays any attention to the shot – and why should they? – he has all night at his disposal to finish me off.

'But this is going to be the catch in it. You will work your way back into the brambles at B. It's all dead stuff, and you can cut out a hole with a pair of garden clippers. Get your legs on soft earth down the badgers' back door and pile their old bedding – there's plenty of it about – underneath your body. You won't be too uncomfortable.

'You will see him long before I do. In fact I shall never see him at all till we've got him. When he raises his revolver or automatic to fire, order him to drop it and put his hands up. He won't. I am sure of that. So you'll have to let him have it with a twelve-bore. I'm afraid he is bound to lose a hand or a foot at that range and I'm not too sure of my law. But I take it we are only using reasonable force when the intention to murder is plain.'

Ian refused to play without the presence of the police. Naturally enough. I had no reason – beyond my own need – to expect him to have preserved a wartime mentality.

'I'll telephone the Chief Constable at once,' he said. 'He's a personal friend. At the Shop with me.'

I replied that I had no objection provided the Chief Constable could, at such short notice, provide us with a policeman guaranteed to lie fairly motionless for four hours and not even slap at a midge for the last two of them. What he would give us would be a detective who was very good indeed at sitting in a car or standing inconspicuously on a street corner.

'But he can trail the man,' Ian said, 'now that you have predicted his movements.'

I ridiculed that. 'Good evening, sir, I am a police officer and it is my duty to inquire your business.' 'I am enjoying the cool of the evening officer.' 'Your name and address?' 'With great pleasure.'

'And he will give it,' I went on, 'the correct address where he *is* staying and the false name he is staying under. But he can't be detained. And he won't be there in the morning. There's not a thing the police can do until they have some evidence of a crime.'

'They can prevent it.'

'They can indeed. But tonight only. And two months later the detective responsible for me is bluffed by a gentleman of obvious respectability who pretends to be the Inspector of Inland Revenue or a Commissioner of Church Lands and calls at half a dozen houses before mine.'

'What about the description? Heavy build? Thick, black eyebrows?'

'He may not have them. I'm doubtful about the eyebrows

58

already. As for the weight – don't you remember Vasile Mavro and his pneumatic stomach?'

Ian smiled at last.

'It took Vasile weeks to learn to walk as if he were really carrying that stomach,' he said. 'After all, this fellow hasn't been trained by us.'

'Hasn't he? If he was in Buchenwald or had friends who were, it's very likely that he was trained by us or some organization nearly as good.'

'But then he can make rings round any county police!' Ian exclaimed.

'Round Special Branch, too – provided that his motive is perplexing, and that he is working alone, not for any political organization. Look at it this way! It was you who first brought up the tiger metaphor. Well, imagine he's an experienced tiger with a taste for man! I gather that the difficulty is to make and keep contact. In fact it can't be done without tying out a bait. That's what I am. I have to be, because we don't know any other which would tempt him. If you or the police refuse to let me hunt him in my own way I shall be killed in his.

'And here's one other point! I'd like to talk to the tiger. Suppose I am the last on the list? The murders of Sporn and Dickfuss are nothing. I'd give him a medal for them. If I think he has finished, if I can convince him who and what I really was, I may not hand him over to the police at all.'

'You have forgotten the postman,' Ian protested.

'Punishing him is not going to bring the postman back to life. That could remain between the tiger and his God, so long as he doesn't force us to send him to hospital.'

It was this argument – the weakest of all – which, I think, persuaded Ian. He had been wavering ever since I suggested the obvious truth that we were dealing with someone who had been a colleague or ally during the war.

'But you're not going to sit on that nest or machan of yours if the tiger is examining it right now,' he said.

'Why not?'

'Thorns. Didn't you say you had considered drawing-pins?'

I assured him that was only panic. No one except a pathologist could do much damage with a surface scratch. And anyway there were no thorns on an alder so why arouse unnecessary suspicion by putting them there?

'What time do I get into position?'

'Let's say he has finished going over the ground now or half an hour ago. Then he will want a meal, because he didn't have any lunch. The sooner you are in position the better, but not later than six.'

The mention of meals at once brought out the regimental officer. Ian reproached himself for not realizing earlier that I had eaten nothing since lunch the day before – in fact I had had plenty, though in bits and pieces – and insisted on bringing back some food before he went to ground with the badgers.

Since I had to give way on the question of bringing in the police somewhere, we agreed that Ian should telephone his friend, using a vague and deprecating English manner, to the effect that it was just possible that he had come upon the trail of the parcel which blew up the postman, and that he should give a description of the suspect.

That was sound sense. If the dark gentleman, wounded or not, got away from us after showing his intention, it was a straight police job to hold him for inquiry until Ian could identify him. It was impossible to guess which way he would go, but, since his line of communication was across the Long Down, a patrol car on the far side of it had a chance of picking him up. Ian was also going to ask for police at the corner where the Stoke road entered Hernsholt. He thought he could manage all that on an old boy basis without giving too much away.

His farm was only some three miles off, so that he was back at half past five with a cold chicken and a bottle of wine. He had been able to arrange that two traffic patrols, in the course of their normal routine, should cover the roads leading away from the Long Down between nine and midnight and should keep an eye on parked cars. He could not get police to watch the Hernsholt end of the Stoke road as well and had detailed the invaluable Isaac Purvis for this duty – with strict orders not to interfere in any way with the big man in the brown suit and to telephone the police immediately if he appeared to be hurt.

Ian was going to leave his car in Stoke and walk from there. His movements could be watched from the firs or the stream as far as the badger fortress but no farther. Once he had rounded that tangle of thorn and bramble he could hack his way into it. Rather belatedly I remembered that he was over fifty, and advised him to leave all violent action to me if there had to be any. He replied that he was a hard-working farmer and far fitter than he had been at the end of the war; he guaranteed to carry me any time a hundred yards further than I could carry him. No, his chief objection to the whole plan was that he had to walk across somebody else's land carrying a gun and couldn't think of any convincing excuse if he met the owner.

I ate my chicken and drank half the bottle. A little after seven there was a sharp, freshening shower. I was glad that Ian, farmer or not, was safely tucked into the badger fortress where hardly a drop would penetrate. The evening turned out to be one of gold and grey, innocently English and less glaring than the previous night which stuck in my mind as black and crimson.

At half past eight I set out and took the field path down from the north, for I was not going to trust myself to the Stoke road. Ian was in position. His field of fire was deadly, but he had made himself a bit too comfortable. The dark hole under dead brambles was obvious as I came along the tiger's expected line of approach. I bent down a branch and tied it inconspicuously so that the leaves drooped across the mouth of the tunnel.

Then I went round the end of the badger fortress and, presumably, into full view of my executioner if he had already returned to the firs or to the bridge. The nearest patch of cover on that side gave him a range of a hundred and forty yards. I felt at first a little naked, in spite of being certain that he wouldn't draw attention to himself by carrying a rifle, and that if he did I should long ago have been found dead in the cottage garden.

I climbed into the alder and sat still. The sun set, and the world became pearl grey. It was such a familiar world. How many times I had watched my gentle, nervous, little mammals under exactly similar conditions! I heard badger cubs yelping underground that it was time to go out. They stopped that very suddenly. A sharp nip from mother had probably impressed upon them that there were two smelly boots down the back door and that long and careful exploration was needed before going out of the front.

Partridges called from the tussocky grass behind me. A Little Owl landed on the hawthorn opposite with what was probably a shrew in his talons. That was the only sign of any violence at all in the hunting dusk. Cows had been let into the field across the stream since the afternoon, and slowly shifted their groupings as they tore at and chewed – most peaceful of sounds – a last bite of the rich grass along the water.

There was no moon, and under the overcast sky the light faded early. I no longer fussed about the range of a hundred and forty yards; what began to matter was how much we two enemies could see at ten. The stream and its boggy edges protected my front. Out to my right there was featureless meadow upon which anything which moved could be spotted. Behind me was rough grass on a slight but uneven slope, terraced and pitted by the paths of sheep and cattle through the winter mud. I felt confident that my trained ears would hear anyone who tried to move over this; and anyway it was partly covered by Ian. To my left and overshadowing me was the black bulk of the badger fortress which smothered all possibility of seeing and listening. The darker it got, the more certain I became that my assassin could not miss the opportunity I had arranged for him and that the trap would work. From moment to moment I expected to hear Ian's challenge and shot.

The tiger was leaving it late. I wondered again how much he knew of naturalists. In the unlikely event of a badger leaving the sett on my side I would only have seen his streak of white. There was no conceivable point in staying up in the alder unless I intended to take flashlight photographs. And I was not carrying a camera.

For distraction I gave the badgers some of my attention. One had possibly crossed the stream and was keeping his usual obstinate course, for a cow blew hard and moved away. That aroused a question in my mind, but thereafter the movements of the cattle were perfectly natural. I could hear the tearing gradually die away as one by one they lay down. Two or three followed the course of the stream and I could just see the black bulks across the water. Out of sight, immediately below the fortress, another squelched through the boggy ground, then passed across my front and vanished.

After that there was absolute silence. I heard Ian cautiously change position. I knew what the faint crackle was, but the tiger could not possibly know – if, that is, he were anywhere near and not enjoying his after-dinner coffee miles away or waiting for me at the Warren. I decided that I had finished with that cottage. It was a good base for attack if the enemy had given me plenty of time to observe him and his ways, but it was hopeless for defence.

I began to feel drowsy and changed position. It did not matter how much noise I made except from the point of view of putting on a convincing act. The muscles beneath my thighs were sore and painful from resting across a narrow branch, so I drew up my feet and squatted knee to chin. From a distance I must have looked like a bulky, shapeless bird roosting dangerously close to the ground.

It was that movement which saved me. Out of the tail end of my eye I saw the silhouette of the lower end of the badger fortress harden, detach itself and charge. There might have been just time to shoot, but shooting had never been in my mind. From my coiled-spring squat I sailed into the air out of the alder and came down feet foremost on to the great dome of thorn and bramble like Brer Rabbit hitting the briar patch. I sank up to my chest, for the moment not noticing at all the little furies of thorns. I thought I was a better target than ever, but I cannot have been. The longer stems of hawthorn opposite my face must have masked me, though I could see clearly through them.

Ian yelled and struggled to get out of his tunnel. The big, dim figure under the alder jumped back, evidently startled that there was another person present. In half a dozen strides he had merged himself again with the darkness at the lower end of the badger fortress, where he seemed to hesitate. Then I heard him splosh across the stream. I just had time and enough sense to whisper to Ian, who was three-quarters out of his hole, that he should talk loudly about frightening the badgers and ask me what the hell I thought I was doing.

It took me a painful ten minutes to extricate myself with the aid of the clippers. I couldn't go up, and I could only sink down by degrees. When at last I was standing on earth, striped all over by superficial scratches, I had to go out feet first by way of Ian's hole.

Why the tiger should have mistrusted the obvious and expected line of approach I did not then know, but I was on the right lines when I wondered how much he had seen of naturalists and their ways. How he had come up was clear. He had very slowly and cautiously moved among the cows, never startling them but gradually shifting them down to the water. That, as Ian pointed out, was not so easy. It was another slight indication that Isaac Purvis's gentleman really did own or farm land.

When one of the cows was squelching through the soft ground he had crossed the stream under cover of its steps and landed on a small patch at the south-east corner of the fortress which was clear of bushes and hidden from the alder. I had entirely overlooked that vital, little sector of turf. Even if there had been cows in the meadow during the afternoon, I am sure that its possibilities would never have occurred to me.

Once safely across he had waited some time to make out my outline. The whole length of the badger fortress was too long a range for a pistol at night. He may have raised and lowered it half a dozen times before deciding that he couldn't afford the risk of missing. When I shifted my legs he thought that I was off home and that his opportunity would be lost. So he charged in. I had no time to drop out of the tree and start running.

While we were looking for his footprints in the mud we came across a charred patch of dead bramble on the edge of the stream where the leaf dust was still smouldering. There was only one conceivable explanation of this. He had stopped for a moment in his escape to light a scrap of paper from his pocket and push it into the dry debris. It didn't work. If he had had time and a newspaper it would have worked. The wind was right. The dead bramble and the old, dry badger-bedding would have gone up and consumed the whole fortress in one roar of flame while I was still stuck in it. Such concentration of cruelty and hatred left us both shaken. I don't think he could have been inspired to fire the bramble on the spur of the moment. I have no doubt at all that he had planned that end for me during the afternoon. A crippling, not a killing shot. Then tie my feet and heave me into the bush. Then light the debris at leisure.

'Still about, do you think?' Ian asked.

'No. He can't tell what may be closing in ahead of him. By God, I hope the police pick him up!'

'At any rate we have enough evidence now.'

But had we? Yes, provided there were good grounds for connecting him with my suburb and the postman, and provided that German police, a day or two later, could prove his presence in Germany at the time of the three executions. Ourselves, we could not prove much. Suppose he claimed that he, too, was interested in badger setts? Suppose he apologized for disturbing us and said that for some unknown reason I seemed very nervous? He could be quite convincing if he had a good excuse for staying in the neighbourhood.

'We shan't hear of him again for some time if he gets clear,' Ian said.

That was true enough. I hardly knew whether to be glad or sorry. It meant that the initiative had once more passed to the tiger and that I should have to start all over again.

I went home with Ian, thankful that he was a bachelor and that I did not have to do any explaining. His reason for never marrying was, I think, not very different from my own – too occupied during the war by the terrible strain of protecting and sometimes sacrificing his agents, and after that too occupied by a sense of guilt.

The police had nothing to report – no man on foot, no parked car on any of the roads leading away from the Long Down. Ian's friend, the Chief Constable, evidently thought that hunches were better left to Scotland Yard.

Isaac Purvis had done rather better by leaning on a cousin's garden fence and quietly ruminating. At half past ten the dark gentleman had passed him, walking quite casually. On reaching the outskirts of Hernsholt he had turned right, away from the village, which made it pretty certain that he was aiming for the safe, deserted expanse of the Long Down and intended to reach it by the path which led round the bottom of my garden.

I slept late on that Friday morning and lay in bed wondering how far pride and shame – in my case difficult to distinguish – had been responsible for this single-handed attempt to protect myself. Yet I had so nearly succeeded. By this move to the country, by the selection of my own ground for the trap and the placing and baiting of it I had come nearer to identifying the assassin than ever could have been done by policemen. And though I had failed I was no worse off than before.

Ian had gone off to Towcester to buy some beef calves, so before lunch I dropped into the Haunch of Mutton, partly to feel a tranquil human society around me, partly to keep in touch with Ferrin.

'You'd be more comfortable in the saloon,' he said. 'You look tired.'

My intelligence was sluggish. I saw no reason why I should be treated as if I were some highly respectable old lady who might not like to take her drink in the public bar. But I obediently followed my beer and the landlord into the so-called saloon – a small room with a table and four prim chairs, vases of artificial flowers on the mantel-piece, and between them a brewer's calendar displaying a bashful young woman in highly improbable underclothing.

'You'll be more private in here,' Ferrin insisted. 'If I can get hold of him, there's someone who might want to talk to you. And then again he might not.'

In a quarter of an hour he returned with an earthy little man whose walk and manner suggested the farm hand, but whose sharp features and sturdy market-town clothes were more in keeping with a small cattle-dealer or auctioneers' clerk.

'This is Jim Melton. Jim, this is the professor,' said Ferrin, setting down Melton's stiff whisky alongside my tankard. 'You ring the bell if you want anything.'

I offered a cigarette and kept the conversation going on the weather and the state of the hay crop until I felt that the conventions of southern English politeness had been satisfied. Then I ventured to say that Colonel Parrow had been looking for him the day before.

'Comes the colonel over me,' said Jim Melton obscurely.

I suggested that it was just an army habit and didn't mean anything.

'That's what *I* say. Don't mean a thing! Thursday week, 'alf past three, Mr Melton. How's a busy man like me to know where he's going to be Thursday week? Now Ferrin here is different. Whenever you're passing, Jim, he says.'

'The Haunch of Mutton is your business address?' I asked.

'Yes and no. Depends on the business. But I'm always glad to oblige Mr Ferrin – especially as he tells me the rozzers would like to know all you know, perfesser.'

It was plain that Ferrin had all the virtues of a second-in-command. He took his chief's instructions and dryly dolled them up to suit the taste of the recipient.

'Not that I've anything against rozzers,' Jim Melton went on. 'We pays 'em, don't we? That's what I says to our little fellow last week when he serves me a summons. It's what I pays yer to do, Jack, I says. But you're wrong as usual.'

'And was he?'

'He's no fool, Jack,' replied Jim Melton non-committally. 'But he don't know his law like I do.'

I rang the bell and had our glasses refilled. Mr Melton was silent for a while, carefully observing me with side-long glances which were no more impolite than those of a bird.

'If Ferrin hadn't told me as you were a perfesser,' he said, 'I'd take my oath you was a gamekeeper, every bit of you.'

I chuckled at his acuteness and explained what I really was – neither one nor the other but a bit of both. Then I remembered that Ian or Ferrin had been serving out science fiction to that old soldier, Isaac Purvis.

'Blood count of the smaller mammals is what I am working

on,' I said mysteriously. 'Fission products in the milk are not clear enough evidence.'

Jim Melton, to my surprise, seemed to know what I was talking about – which was more than I did myself.

'It was them atom bombs which put an end to the rabbits,' he said. 'Myxomatosis they calls it, and what I says is: it comes from all them atom products fallin' down their floppy ear'oles. I ought to get compensation. Trappin' was one of my businesses.'

'Well, I suppose you can still find a bit of sport?'

Mr Melton looked shocked, but surrendered when he saw that I was not.

'I can,' he admitted. 'But I only tells you that, mind, to give you confidence. And I don't hold with them dirty gangs from London what clears out all the pheasants in one night. I'm a reasonable man. One for the pot, and one for my expenses.'

I rang the bell for Ferrin again. I have always respected the sporting, single-handed poacher and employed him if he were employable at all. Jim Melton was a useful ally.

'Heard of Fred Gorble?' he asked, when more drinks were on the table.

'No.'

'Fred ain't too careful what he buys, see? Lives in a caravan on a bit of woodland of his own, with some old farm buildings and no proper road to 'em. I puts some honest business his way from time to time, which makes a nice change for him.

'Tuesday night I was up there to tell 'im about a load of old iron what he might have a use for when I sees a 'orse in the stable what I wasn't meant to see. Tidy 'orse that, I says. Not mine, says he. Whose is it, I asks, for I knows an old girl out Blixworth way what's looking for a quiet 'orse up to her weight. You forget about that 'orse, Jim, he says – you ain't seen it.

'Well, I thinks, that 'orse is a 'unter if ever I see one, but what's he up to with a 'unter in the flat season? If it had been winter, I'd have known he was keeping it till the dye wore off. So I thinks, what's in this for me? Just as you would yourself. And when I says good-bye to Fred, I don't go far but slips round the back of the wood, like. I watches him looking for me, 'alf-'earted, but he soon gives up his suspicions.

'Now, this is what I sees, and I wouldn't think nothing of it if Ferrin hadn't said you was a friend of his and that you weren't trustin' the rozzers to tell you all *they* knows any more than you want to tell them all *you* knows.

'Bloke comes along about 'alf past nine and goes into Fred's from the back. Changes into boots and breeches and bowler 'at and then goes off on the 'orse. Funny time for hackin', I thinks. And that's all I knows.'

'When you saw him go into Gorble's from the back,' I asked, 'could he have been coming from the Long Down?'

'Not your end of it, he couldn't. But the other end he could.'

'How was he dressed before he changed?'

'Couldn't see in the dusk. But a big bloke, he was, with a cap on his head.'

'Any form of luggage? A knapsack on his back?' I asked, for I couldn't understand how he had managed to change out of riding kit and into the brown tweed suit at Fred Gorble's.

'Rolled cape on his saddle when I saw him,' Jim Melton suggested.

That was good enough. All he needed to carry in the roll were shoes, a cap, a pair of trousers to match his jacket and a collar and tie to take the place of his cravat.

This invaluable agent now insisted on paying for the next round of drinks. Stiff whiskies seemed to have no effect on him whatever. Myself, I was awash with beer; but Ian's brewery did not seem to be all Ferrin claimed for it. When he had finished, Jim Melton nodded to me, vanished through the kitchen door of the pub, round the back of the yard into the road and along the road to the public bar. It was very evidently his habit to let no one know his business or whereabouts.

As soon as Ian came home I told him the story. He went straight to the telephone to ask whether a rider had passed either of the patrol cars the night before.

'That damned Melton!' he exclaimed while he waited for the reply. 'I've spent all of a week trying to get hold of him to tell him to keep his eyes open. Bloody little crook! Doesn't he strike you as the perfect type of double agent?'

He didn't. Jim had no sense of self-importance. All he wanted from life was to be allowed to scrabble around among the roots of it and avoid notice.

'What *did* he do in the war?' I asked.

'Caught rats for the Ministry of Agriculture – after fooling the psychiatrists into believing he had fits every time he heard a bang.'

'And the village didn't give him away?'

'Not they! The joke kept 'em happy for five years!'

I could see that Jim Melton would be for ever beyond Ian's understanding. He had the quality of an old-fashioned Central European peasant. Any and all rascality was forgivable so long as it made established authority look an ass. The Meltons are the only relic of the feudal system left in England.

The call from the Chief Constable came through. Yes, one of the patrol cars had passed a well-dressed man on a horse and paid no attention.

'Did they stop?' I asked.

No, they had not stopped – just seen him in the headlights as they cruised by.

The dark gentleman had played his formidable knowledge of customs and country for all it was worth. Hunting with the famous packs of the Whaddon Chase and the Grafton was the winter sport of the district, and horse-breeding a flourishing local industry. Men in cars and on foot might be worth watching, but a well-dressed man on a horse would be assumed to have no interest in vulgar crime. He would not even arouse the curiosity of a town-bred traffic cop, whereas a local farmer would at least wonder where the devil he was hacking to or from at that time of night.

He must have discovered Fred Gorble's establishment in his first reconnaissance of the district – for it would be an inconceivable coincidence that they already knew each other. Then he coolly rode in, weighed him up, told him a good story and arranged to stable his horse at a price which would keep Gorble's mouth shut. The choice of a horse for transport between his base and the approaches to the Long Down was a stroke of genius. Should an unfortunate incident at the Warren be discovered before he was clear of the district, he could either canter casually past the police or, at the worst, make a highwayman's escape across country.

'Well, now straight to the police!' said Ian briskly. 'They can get on his tail and establish his identity. Where did he hire his horse? Where was he staying?'

'He hired his horse under a false name,' I answered, perhaps impatiently. 'And wherever he was staying, he's not there now. He may even be having lunch in your club today – without his prominent black eyebrows.'

'All right, Charles, all right! But how did he travel? Taxi-drivers, ticket-collectors, car registration numbers – that's all daily bread and butter to the police.'

'Yes. They will trace him up to a point. But they won't get near his identity.'

'He isn't a superman!'

I agreed that he was not. He was just trained – and so was I – to recognize, anticipate, and avoid police. I never, in old days, took a taxi anywhere near my starting point. I always gave the driver a reasonable mass destination which was close to, but not my real one. I never repeated the same route. There would be no trouble in tracing the man to Euston Station, and a complete blank when he left it.

'But you can't do nothing!' Ian exclaimed – and then, feeling that despairing cries were not strong enough, added: 'You must not do nothing!'

I begged him to look at the position from my opponent's point of view – who could not know that I had discovered the drugged dog nor that I suspected him. So the trap did not quite make sense as a trap.

'Was it one at all?' I went on. 'Well, I had a friend with me whom he never saw arrive. And he had some other strongish reason – I don't know what – to smell a rat. So for his own safety he must assume I expected him. And therefore it is dead certain he has cleared right out of the district for the moment and covered his tracks.

'But there are also some good arguments against it being a trap. The friend was with me because I don't like being alone. The friend shouted and struggled to get out but said nothing which could definitely prove I was not quietly following my profession and watching badgers. All the time he has been here he has not seen a sign of the police, in uniform or out of it. The car which passed him on the road meant no more than any other cruising police car.

'So what is his next move in this game where he cannot see the other board, but the referee has said "Check"? He must make up his mind by what I do. It is certain that I myself know that a murderous attack was made on me, whatever excuse I may have given to my unknown friend. Consequently I must show nervousness and run. That's the surest way of getting him to follow.'

Ian would not listen. He became more and more regimental. He insisted on telling the whole story to the police, and that I should stay with him while they made their investigations.

'I've been thinking all day what would have happened if I had been forced to put a charge of shot into that fellow last night,' he said. 'I know he deserves it. But the police should have known exactly what we were doing.'

'And forbidden it or wrecked it.'

'That's their funeral.'

'Mine, too, unfortunately.'

'Very well. But it's against common sense and it's against my – my –'

I was certain he was going to say 'orders'.

'– Against my principles. I cannot help you any more, Charles, unless you allow me to keep the police informed.'

I said I had told him a dozen times why I wouldn't. Because I would not be guarded. Because I did not want my shadow questioned, frightened off and returning months later when I was not expecting him. Because this was a private matter between me and him.

'For which you are quite likely to be publicly sentenced to death.'

That was my own business, I replied. Would he promise to

leave the police out of it if I never asked anything more from him?

He agreed to that. He was very unhappy but obstinate. It was all my fault. I should have recognized that he was not the same man as in the war, and that it had become for him, as for the rest of us, a mere episode breaking the continuity of an orderly life. Both of us, as I have indicated, found the special beastliness of that episode still too much in the present. It is hard for a man of scrupulous mercy and humanity to be forced into the morals of a ruthless gangster. But he had the pattern to carry him along – a continuity of landed gentry into army and back to landed gentry. I had no pattern.

So there was nothing for it but to go on alone. Against Ian I felt not the slightest resentment. I had most unfairly dragged him into my affairs by playing upon whatever trace of romanticism remained in him; the point at which my plan was bound to appear to him sheer irresponsibility was soon reached. But I could not help feeling rejected. What I wanted was impossible – to repeat war, to know, as it were, that at least in London I was honoured and trusted. And London and Ian had been the same thing.

I did not know what to do. To mark time and be careful were all I *could* do. I decided to return to my cottage for the night. My opponent, whatever his source of intelligence, could hardly spot the single night I had passed with Ian; but if I stayed longer he might get on to it. I did not want him to find out that I had been accompanied by such a formidable friend at the badger sett. Ian's past was well known.

All the surroundings of Hernsholt now seemed to me puzzling and unfriendly; they refused, like so much at the heart of England, to be defined. Forest when seen from ground level. The tamest farming country when seen from the top of a tree. How was I to go to work within these subtle enclosures of life as well as fields? I admired that cruel devil who thought that burning alive was the right death for me. He was able to find his way through subtleties single-handed and confidently, backed by his money and – of this I was now certain – an impregnable social position.

My own affinities with Jim Melton, I reflected sourly, were probably closer than with Ian and his kind – though whether that was because I had been brought up to laugh at the middle classes and their obsession with legal forms or because I was a fish out of water I could not decide.

Thought of Jim Melton reminded me that he was better than nothing; indeed he might be better than anything. I walked over to see Ferrin and found him building a greenhouse in the garden behind his pub when he certainly ought to have been weeding his vegetables. He was that sort of gardener.

I asked him where I could find Jim Melton.

'Predestination, that's what it is,' he answered dryly. 'The more I live round here, the more I'm certain nobody has any free will except me. Blowed if I don't write to the *Church Times* about it one day! Jim said to me after you left that you'd be asking for him some time soon, and if you did I was to send you round to his cottage.'

He gave me Jim's address. It was a yellow-brick council house on the road to Stony Stratford. I should have expected him to live in a derelict gamekeeper's cottage in the middle of nowhere.

'Not he!' Ferrin said. 'You wouldn't catch Jim putting up with an old-fashioned place if he could work himself into a new one with the ratepayers paying half his rent for him.'

'I want an hour or two of his time. It will be expensive, I suppose?'

'That's for Jim to say. But I don't mind telling you, Mr Dennim, he's taken a liking to you.'

'I wonder why.'

'Ever seen an animal you couldn't get on with?'

'Lots.'

'One that was free to be got on with, if you see what I mean.'

I did. It was well put. I certainly do not offend tame animals, and I have noticed – though the observation is worthless since it cannot be measured by statistics – that by wild creatures my presence, even when it is known, seems to be easily accepted. But I do not wish to sound like some dear old lady who claims that all her cats love her. Why in the world shouldn't they?

'Well, Jim, he doesn't think,' Ferrin went on, 'not what you and I would call thinking. He believes in his comfort, mind you, and when it comes to a deal he's sharp. But he couldn't tell you what makes him tick any more than his jackdaw could.'

The jackdaw was first with a greeting when I opened Jim Melton's garden gate. It furiously attacked my ankles, pecked the hand I put down and then walked straight up my arm on to my shoulder.

Two small female Meltons, who were busy filling a doll's pram with water, regarded this with interest.

'Mind yer ear, mister,' one said.

This was suspiciously like a word of command to the jackdaw, which gave me a sharp nip.

'Didn't say no more than damn-you,' complained the other little girl, disappointed.

'What do visitors usually say?' I asked.

I was told. I wouldn't have inquired if I could have guessed what was going to come out of those rosebud mouths.

'Thought you might be along, perfesser,' said Jim Melton, appearing from the back of the house.

The jackdaw danced on my shoulder and repeated the expression it had just heard. The sounds were not really intelligible, though it made a fair shot at the word 'bastard'.

'And if I am, what the hell's it got to do with you?' Jim said. 'You mind yer own business! Mother!'

Mrs Melton came out of the front door. She was oddly dressed in a very dirty but quite well-fitting coat and skirt. The coat was longer than was fashionable and faintly suggested 1914. Her grey-streaked, tan-coloured hair was the same shade as her face, apart from the red on her cheek bones. The coat and the colouring strongly suggested English gipsy blood.

'Can't offer you a drink,' Jim apologized. 'She won't 'ave a drop in the house.'

Mrs Melton and I shook hands and exchanged smiles. The prohibition was probably wise. Then she sorted out the Miss Meltons with some proper remarks on language before gentlemen. The water in the doll's pram turned out to be a time-and-motion experiment; it was easier to take the bath to the puppy than the puppy, who didn't like it, to the bath. But the pram leaked. I suggested the old fairy-tale remedy of stopping it with moss and daubing it with clay. Mrs Melton, who was just leading up to all the usual mother's remarks about playing with water, had from politeness to leave them unsaid.

All this seemed to have acted as sufficient introduction, so when I was alone with Jim I went straight to the point.

'Where did he hire his horse?'

'Now, that's just what I asks after you and me had our little talk,' Jim replied, 'because if I knew enough about that 'orse to tell the old girl out Blixworth way that it was quiet and going cheap, I'd be doing a favour to you *and* meself.'

He gave me a horse-coper's wink which dated from the last century and waited for questions. I said that I supposed he knew most of the livery stables within easy riding of Fred Gorble's place.

'I do. And that's as much as to say I know where the 'orse didn't come from. So I guessed where he did. Right second time! He 'ired that 'orse from Boscastle's stables in Woburn.'

Jim had turned up at the stables soon after lunch. Having a perfect excuse for inquiries, he had been able to show as much interest in the hirer as the horse.

The well-dressed stranger had given his name as Mr fforde-Crankshaw. He had been fussy about the spelling with two little 'f's; otherwise his manner was unassuming and natural. fforde-Crankshaw was a fine invention, I thought – in character, impressive, but not too impressive.

He had hired the horse on the excuse of getting his weight down. Every morning he turned up about nine, rode off and came back before dark. As he paid well, was an experienced horseman and never brought his mount in tired, the proprietor of the livery stables was not worried and would indeed have been delighted – being short of competent staff – to let him exercise his horses free of charge.

Generally he had telephoned for a taxi and caught a ten-thirty train back to London. But on Wednesday night he had not returned till long after eleven, explaining that he had been dining with friends and that the horse had been well looked after; he had then taken a taxi to Watford and presumably picked up a train there.

Last night – Thursday night – he had ridden in still later. After saying that he might not be back for some days he had simply vanished while the horse was being unsaddled. The stables did not know how he had returned to London and supposed he had been given a lift by a friend.

I found nothing specially mysterious in that. It was common sense to disappear and cover his tracks when he could not tell exactly what trap he had escaped and whether it was a trap at all. I guessed that he had walked to the A5 road and got himself home from there – though it seemed risky. That, if any.. where, was where the police block would be.

'Where's the spade, Dad?' asked the elder daughter, interrupting us.

'Back of the shed. Under them mole traps.'

'No, 't ain't. And we want to dig some clay like the gentleman told us.'

'Well, if 't ain't, it's where you blasted little darlin's put it. Last Saturday they slings all their old dolls in a bonfire,' he went on, 'and near burns up the pitchfork till their ma has to tell 'em that girls aren't never devils. Not in 'Ell, that is.'

Mrs Melton called us all in to eat sausage and mash, the jackdaw on the table and helping with the mash. She asked no questions. She could mind her own business as well as her husband. They must have been certain of their daughters, too, for they did not care what was revealed in front of them.

'What we want to know now,' said Jim, 'is what excuse he gave old Fred Gorble for leaving the 'orse there all day. Him and his two little "f"s! Two big uns I'd call him!'

'I'll get that out of Fred,' Mrs Melton remarked.

There must have been long agreement between Mr and Mrs Melton as to their respective sphere of operations. Her offer, without another word, seemed to open his eyes.

'Women!' he exclaimed. 'Fred's no fool, and he don't like standing up in the box any more than anyone else. That fforde-Crankshaw, he comes ridin' in looking as stately as a Master of 'Ounds and not troublin' his 'ead about crime what you'd call crime. So what could he have told Fred? That he was out tom-cattin' of course! He didn't want anyone to know as he'd been over this way, and especially not her 'usband. I'll drive the missus round to Fred, and she'll get it out of him like she said she would.'

After supper Mrs Melton put on a formidable hat, and we went across the kitchen garden to the shed – a store or ammunition hut which Jim had picked up from the army and now served as garage and barn. Its long axis was set obliquely to the cottage and the door faced more or less up the road.

Inside were piles of useful junk and an incredible vehicle with a shining bonnet – black, powerful, looking as if it were an amateur conversion of one of the royal laudaulettes into a van.

'It's a 'earse,' Jim explained. 'Comes a bit 'ard on petrol. But that's an income tax expense. I'm a farmer, see? Got more than five acres, I have, here and there.'

Mr and Mrs Melton got in, and the hearse burst out into the road. It was Jim's method of entering and leaving his garage and may have accounted for the angle at which he set it. No doubt he compensated for his dislike of military service by imagining himself a cowboy in a hurry or a cavalier carrying news to the king.

I was left to entertain the Miss Meltons. A shower drove us indoors and limited the amusements I could provide. There was not a book in the house, so we turned to a paint-box. Caricatures of authority in the shape of school teachers and policemen were so popular that for an hour there was silence except for recommendations to make the backside bigger or the nose redder.

Our peace was broken by the jackdaw's strident call of greeting. The bird seemed to be acting efficiently as watchdog till the new puppy grew up. One of the Miss Meltons looked out of the front window, but there was nobody about. The rain had just started to pelt down and heavy thunder clouds had brought an early dusk.

'Practising – that's what he's doing,' she said, 'unless someone has brought the spade back.'

'Dad's hid it so we can't bust it,' replied the other contemptuously. 'Who's goin' to walk mile 'n' 'alf to borrow a spade?'

No one. I agreed. But if somebody was already here and saw the spade, I could imagine a use for it. Impossible, however. I could not be traced to the Meltons' cottage. The connexion between myself and Jim was absolutely undiscoverable – unless the dark stranger hadn't gone to London at all and had been hanging around Hernsholt that very day. And I knew he had not. There would have been an immediate report to Ferrin, and from Ferrin to Ian or me.

'Is there anything like a tip of loose rubbish or a sandpit near here?' I asked.

'Top of the slope behind the shed. Good sand, too. Dad'll sell you a load if you want it.'

I got up and drew the curtains. Jackdaw's chatter and missing spades were no evidence of anything at all. All the same, I did not intend to go out until Jim was back with us. If meanwhile somebody knocked at the door and asked for shelter from the rain – there was no earthly reason why he shouldn't – I would have to get the children out of the room and tell him to keep his hands up while we talked.

It was nearly ten before the Meltons returned – with the same technique. I never even heard Jim change down. He reined the hearse back on its haunches with six inches between the bumpers and a wheelbarrow.

Mr and Mrs Melton were thoroughly relaxed by double whiskies, and cackling over their success. On arrival at Gorble's retreat, Jim had kept firmly in his part of driver, saying that he wouldn't come in, that his old woman wouldn't confide in him what it was all about and he didn't want to know either.

As soon as she was alone with Fred, Mrs Melton told him that a lady had given her an urgent message for he-knew-who. Gorble showed no surprise which proved that she was on the right lines. He said that the gentleman wasn't coming back.

Mrs Melton had then clothed herself in vague gipsy portentousness and delivered a warning that no good would come of it all. She invented a husband who was due back unexpectedly on Saturday from the Assizes. I gathered from her incoherent chuckles that he hadn't been in the dock but was one of Her Majesty's Judges.

This frightened Gorble into indecision. He admitted that he could pass a message, but refused. It wasn't worth his while, he said. The gentleman had paid him well, and there was more money promised if orders were obeyed. Fred expected to receive a telephone call – he wouldn't say where or when – and was forbidden to open his mouth at all except to give the answers to two questions: yes or no.

Eventually, to get rid of her, he told her what the two questions were. Had anybody been making inquiries? Was a certain person still living where he did?

'Ah, him at the Warren!' Mrs Melton exclaimed.

That apparently satisfied Gorble that she knew more about the business than he did. He said he didn't care to be hanging around Hernsholt asking silly questions, and would she get the information for him?

The pair of them waved away my thanks and apologized for stopping on the road. They reckoned I'd be glad to see them.

'We 'aven't give him no trouble,' protested the elder daughter. 'We've been 'aving fun.'

'Aye. In the shed. I can see that,' said Jim severely. 'One day you'll get 'urt burrowin' in all that junk.'

'What's the matter with the shed?' I asked.

'Knocked down a tarpaulin and bust a flower pot.'

'Let's go and see.'

As soon as I had Jim outside, I told him we had never been in the shed and stopped him going straight to it.

'Did you lock the door when you put the van away?'

'I did. Somebody in there, you think?'

It was most unlikely; but if the rain had driven an observer down into the shed for shelter, Jim's sudden and dashing return would certainly have startled him. He had no time to get out of the door but he could have dived into the litter of odds and ends at the back.

'Switch the light on,' I said, 'and don't come any further.

And don't say anything which could give away what we're doing – make out we're looking for a handy plank.'

I did not tell him that I needed him as a witness in case I had to fire in self-defence. I knew he distrusted the box as much as the dock.

Jim switched on the light and I walked through his stores with my hand in my pocket. There was indeed a broken flower pot on the floor, and a tarpaulin had fallen – if that wasn't its usual place – on the top of two upright rolls of wire. Behind them was possible cover for a man provided nobody looked for him.

'This will do the job,' I said, extracting a piece of four by two from a pile of loose timber.

We shut the shed and went out. And yet I felt my enemy. That is difficult to analyse. I suppose that only years of living on one's nerves can teach the difference between imagination which is out of control and the quite dependable instinct of the hunted.

The instinct at any rate was strong enough for me to search about for some logical reason which could justify it. I asked what the stables at Woburn were like.

Jim described a Victorian farmhouse with its back facing a yard round which, on the other three sides, were stables and cow sheds with a second storey of lofts over them.

'When you were leading them on to tell you about fforde-Crankshaw, where actually were you?'

'Bang under the gable with the clock in it.'

'What's up there?'

'Nothing except rats, I'd say.'

It was a far-fetched theory; but what about that vanishing while the horse was being unsaddled? If Mr fforde-Crankshaw were wanted by name or description, the last place the police would look for him would be the livery stables. And if he had decided to lie up there for a day he could probably see and possibly overhear all visitors to the yard.

'When you were talking to the chaps there, did you give your address?'

'They know it,' Jim replied. 'Ah, but didn't I? Bought a nice load of manure, you see. Mushroom farmers, they'll pay any-thing for well-rotted stuff. Yes, they had a new man, and I told him the nearest way.'

It was working out. fforde-Crankshaw, scenting danger but partially convinced he was imagining it, must have been very tempted to check up. There had been no police inquiries, but who was Jim? What was behind his interest?

There was one grave objection to this picture of my oppo-nent's board. He must have calculated on leaving the stable lofts after dark. Yet he had left in broad daylight. Was that possible without being seen and inviting questions?

'What's behind the gable with the clock in it?'

'Company director's place it was once,' Jim said, 'before he went bust and 'ad to run for it with all the money he'd lost farming. Other side of the stables is all his fancy trees and rhododendrons.'

That too fitted. It was now worthwhile to test the only avail-able fact which could prove my hypothesis – or, if not worth-while, it had to be done. I told Jim to stay where he was, and I would find his missing spade for him. I would have liked to have him alongside me, but it was not a fair risk for the father of a family – even though I was pretty sure the tiger would not have returned to the sand-pit from which he could no longer see anything at all.

I crawled up the slope behind the shed and put my head cautiously over the edge of the depression. The working floor of sand, some eight or nine feet beneath me, was bare and the light still good enough to distinguish any object on the flat surface. The spade was there all right.

To see anything else I should have to go down with a torch. That was asking for trouble, since I could not know what was on the opposite side of the excavation; so I contented myself with taking a close look at the wet packed sand within a few feet of my nose. I found fresh footmarks – of a rather pointed shoe which certainly did not belong to any of the Melton family. For the weight of the tiger it was a small foot. The tracks pointed straight for the shed until they were wiped out by the furrows of my knees and forearms.

It was all very interesting, but of no immediate use. Tiger impulsively but sensible reconnoitres Jim's cottage from above. Finds convenient sandpit for observation post. Hunch pays off, for he hasn't been there long before he sees me arrive. Is tempted by spade which he can approach without being seen. A bad mistake, though doubtless it would help if my body wasn't found for a week. Shelters from rain in shed. Could easily have explained that was just what he was doing and got away with it. But his reconstruction of my unseen board is alarming. And Jim is still an enigma. So when he is nearly caught he first hides and then clears out.

'Your spade is in the sandpit,' I told Jim. 'Get it in the morning.'

'Not now?'

'Not now.'

'When you went into the shed, I noticed you kept your 'and in your pocket,' he said. 'Now it's none of my business what you got in it. And what Ferrin tells me is all lies. And me and the colonel, we don't get on. But if you feel lonely up at the Warren, you've only got to say.'

I assured him that I was only going to stay there that night, and it was unlikely I should be disturbed.

'And what do you want the missus to tell Fred?' he asked.

'That nobody has made any inquiries about the rider, and that I left the Warren in a hurry.'

I gratefully accepted his offer to drive me home, and said good-bye to Mrs Melton and the children. The front seat of the hearse was luxurious. It was a remarkable vehicle. The panels all round the body, where plate glass had been, were filled in by neatly overlapping planks attached by angle brackets to the black-and-gold pillars, and varnished black to match. The roof was of stout canvas on bentwood ribs. It made a discreet and efficient van for shifting livestock or any of Jim's less reputable bargains.

'Got it dirt cheap,' he said. 'There ain't no market for used 'earses. And the bloke threw in some nice elm boards for the conversion.'

I avoided offering a silhouette against the naked electric

bulbs in the cottage porch and the shed, and kept well down in my seat until we were out on the road. Yet somehow I knew that it was utterly impossible for the tiger to be about, though my mind, very tired by now, could not see on what I based this certainty.

As we drove towards Hernsholt I ran over the probabilities again and at last got at what was bothering me. If the shelterer from the rain had dived for the cover of those two rolls of wire on Jim's sudden arrival, how had he ever got out of the shed? He had no chance of escaping under the eyes of both Mr and Mrs Melton and Jim had locked the door behind him. So there was something as wrong and incredible as a conjuring trick.

And then I saw it. By all that unriddling of the unintelligible I had been distracted from what was perfectly plain and obvious. I slid instantly off the front seat and fitted as much of my body as I could into the floor of the cab, putting a finger on my lips as a sign to Jim to notice nothing.

'Drive for the nearest lights and police station,' I whispered. 'Don't stop on any account! If anything happens to me, keep going!'

He looked at me in astonishment. I jerked my thumb at the shiny black boards behind the driving seat. He thought for a second and saw what I meant. There was only one place where fforde-Crankshaw could be. When he heard us coming back to the shed and unlocking the door, he had quietly taken refuge in the van. And he was still in it – with nothing but a wooden panel between me and his gun.

There was no means of covering all of myself. If he fired a burst through the partition at the level of heart and lungs he would miss; but if he aimed below where my waist ought to be he would almost certainly score on my head or shoulders. I never felt so coldly exposed. As for slowing down or stopping – that, I thought, would give him just the chance he was waiting for in order to let me have it, jump out and vanish. He was hardly likely to take action while Jim continued to bucket over country roads at a steady forty-five. The only comfort was that if he missed me I could be out of the front seat as quickly as he could drop from the double door at the back, and at last shoot to kill without fear of the law.

It was the devil of an indecisive position. Jim had turned east, and in another two or three minutes we were going to hit the A5 road. He might be able to swing straight into the traffic stream without stopping, but we could not count on it. At that time of night there was usually a procession of lorries passing between London and the west Midlands.

It was the hearse's horn which got us through. It had a deeply respectful note – funereal but commanding enough to make all long-distance lorry drivers jam on their brakes and curse the amateur. Jim halted for a second at the junction. He could not turn right to Bletchley, as we had intended, but he could – just – turn left for Stony Stratford, forcing a truck into the middle of the road and leaving a line of angrily winking headlights behind us. We may very well have given the impression of criminals escaping with the week's wage packets.

'Only one lot of traffic lights now,' Jim whispered. 'I'll jump 'em if you say so. But if you're going to 'and over to the police, what's your 'urry?'

I explained that I dared not give him a safe chance to jump out.

'How thick are those boards?' I asked.

'Thick enough to keep him in.'

'He's only got to open the doors at the back.'

' 'E can't.'

'Why not?'

'Because there ain't no 'andle on the inside. Passengers don't need it, like. Not if the coffin's nailed down proper.'

I remember bursting into a bark of laughter, which I suppose was partly hysterical. So the tiger was as helplessly caught as if he had been a real tiger! It wouldn't do him any good to kill. Nothing would do him any good. He was on his way to the cage or the taxidermist in a plain, black-varnished box-trap.

The line of lights on the main street of Stony Stratford was just ahead when a police car passed us, pulled across in front and signalled to Jim to stop.

Two of the cops closed in on us, one at my door and one at

Jim's. They were very evidently prepared to tell us that whatever we said was, was not. What has made British police adopt their new fashion of weary brutality? Forced on them by criminals or borrowed from alien films? At any rate I did not trust them to take my story seriously. I wanted an inspector at a desk.

At first they accused Jim of not stopping at a Halt Sign. When he insisted that he did stop, they dropped the effort to make him confess he didn't and merely warned him not to take chances. It was pretty clear that the lorry driver who reported us had been a sport and had contented himself with abusing our road sense and our suspicious-looking vehicle.

While one of them examined Jim's papers, the other ordered me to get out and open up the van.

'Open it yourself!' I said. 'And stand behind the door while you do it!'

The van was empty. A flap of the canvas roof hung down, neatly cut out with a knife. The tiger had escaped without even the necessity for any acrobatics. Notches and joints on the corner posts, to which the ornate canopy had once been attached, provided easy footholds. Either at the junction with the main road or now while the police were lecturing us he had climbed up, quietly and decisively chosen his moment and slid to the ground at the back of the van.

I looked up the road. There on the other side of it was his unmistakable figure walking fast but casually past the first of the street lamps. He waved to a bus turning out of a corner ahead. Naturally it did not wait, but that gave him an excuse to hurry. I pointed at him and may have even opened my mouth to shout 'Stop him!' But my arm dropped. What was the use? How in an instant could I persuade those pompous young cops that it was I, not he, who was a law-abiding citizen?

And what charge could I bring? I had not the slightest proof that he had ever been in the van. Jim had never seen his face. I – well, all I could swear after these days and nights of anxiety at the Warren, at the badger fortress and on the road was that I had once observed him out on a quiet country walk. No, for my own safety it was wiser at this point not to reveal that I suspected him. When we met again he could no longer take me by surprise, for I had seen his face and he still did not know it.

I put no limit at all to his daring, but I could safely put a limit to his endurance since he was my own age. So when Jim at last left me at the Warren, I locked the door, relaxed, and cheerfully damned the consequences. I had not been in the cottage for nearly thirty-six hours. The letter from Admiral Cunobel, to which Aunt Georgina had referred, was there waiting for me; it was a warm and genial invitation to come over and stay whenever I liked and for as long as I could.

I felt free to do so, at any rate for a week. I was determined not to involve Georgina and a stranger – even if he had rocked my cradle – in my affairs, but it seemed improbable that my follower could soon begin again to pad along my trail. I had to be found. His careful reconnaissance had to be made.

3

HIDE AND SEEK

NEXT morning I telephoned to the admiral and embarked on one of those very English cross-country journeys which delight me. There is no silence which sings so noticeably in the ears as that of a remote railway junction in the middle of meadows with no village in sight when the noise of the departing train has died away.

Admiral Cunobel had chosen for his retirement a grey-stone Jacobean farmhouse on the southern tip of the Cotswolds, where he seemed entirely contented with village affairs and his garden. Chipping Marton struck me as a livelier spot than Hernsholt. It was linked with the world whereas the Midland village, though not far from London, was lost in pastures. Its first inhabitants had not merely collected together into a Saxon lump; they had built their solid, stone houses in full consciousness of geography. Go downhill on one side and you came to the Severn Estuary. Go downhill on the other and you hit the road from London to Bristol.

The admiral ran the place. He considered it his duty. Chipping Marton, on the other hand, had no use whatever for naval discipline, though it respected energy. Cunobel and his village seemed to live in a state of mutual and exasperated affection.

He drove me home from the station, gave me a drink and then took me round to the vicarage. Georgina was shelling peas in the kitchen. Nur Jehan was also in the kitchen – all fourteen hands of him, coloured much as a Siamese cat except that his magnificent tail was deep cream. He breathed down the back of Georgina's neck with heavy sentimentality.

Georgina pushed his head aside and kissed me on both cheeks, putting an unexpected warmth into her usual formal salutation.

'My dear Charles!' she exclaimed. 'I do hope I didn't alarm you.'

'Not in the least. But if you were in front of the stove instead of the sink and he butted you . . .'

'What I said on the telephone, I mean. I felt afterwards I might have exaggerated the situation.'

'Georgi, it could *not* be exaggerated,' said the admiral indignantly.

Nur Jehan, observing that our attention was engaged, took a hearty mouthful from the bowl of peas and blew the rest on the floor.

'In some ways it certainly could not,' Georgina replied. 'I draw the line at that damned horse in the kitchen, and I shall have the back-door latch replaced by a mortice lock.'

'Do it myself!' said the admiral. 'I'll come down with a screwdriver tonight. But you can cope, Georgi – always could! It's that girl I'm sorry for.'

'Which girl?' I asked.

'Benita, his daughter. She shouldn't have to chuck everything and come down here to the rescue every three months.'

'I have noticed, Peregrine,' said my aunt, 'that long service behind the mast or whatever it is produces an unnatural view of women.'

'Well, my dear, you must admit that she does come down to the rescue.'

'A mere refusal to face her duty to herself, which is to make a career. Miss Gillon, Charles, very sensibly decided on a profession instead of resigning herself to becoming a mamby pamby old maid in the country. She has a gift for vulgar drawing and is employed by advertising agencies.'

'You mean a vulgar gift for drawing, Georgi.'

'I mean just what I say, Peregrine. I consider some of her drawings extremely vulgar and not at all funny. She is obsessed by desert islands. And I do wish you would not interrupt. Benita does not like London. And I am forced to the conclusion that she frequently comes down to rescue her father when he does not need rescuing at all.'

I was faintly suspicious. My aunt had never said a word about the vicar's daughter or perhaps she had passed so lightly over the name that I assumed it belonged to some loyal parishioner.

I had been somewhat too occupied to remember the admiral's staunch feeling for the proprieties. Since he wouldn't put Georgina up himself because of the absence of any female relative, it stood to reason that the vicar – whom I knew to be a widower – must have the essential woman in residence.

The admiral's vicar came in from the garden, bringing with him a lot of mud and some vague and hearty apologies. I liked him at once. He had merry eyes and an air of almost Bohemian preoccupation. I mean that his disregard for the things of this world was casual rather than saintly.

He was full of praise of my aunt, who, he said, was an excellent influence on all of them – all of them. Nur Jehan appeared to resent being included or, more probably, felt that the vicar's pat on entering the kitchen had been insufficient. He gently nipped his owner's shoulder.

'Pure Persian Arab,' Matthew Gillon explained to me proudly. 'A parishioner of mine brought him home from Kerman where he had been vice-consul. Nur Jehan comes from the Kerman desert and as a foal he was brought up in the family tent, which I believe is very usual. So when my friend settled here he had not the heart to keep him out of the house. I do not think he wished to. Both his boys had been killed in the war, and the stallion, I'm afraid, was all he had left to love. A lonely man. After only a year in our midst he passed away, leaving me this superb young three-year-old. So I did not like to change Nur Jehan's habits too suddenly. Poor fellow, he deeply felt the loss of his father – his owner, I mean.'

'He is completely untrained,' Georgina said severely. 'He gets out of the Glebe meadow and terrifies the village children, let alone passing motorists.'

'I'm getting on with the fences as fast as I possibly can single-handed, Mrs Dennim,' the vicar protested weakly. 'And you yourself advised me to remember the – ah – stud fees.'

'Georgi, don't tell me you're encouraging him in this folly!' the admiral accused her. 'And when you know very well that this wretched stallion . . .'

'I don't agree at all,' Aunt Georgina interrupted. 'Nur Jehan is merely a late developer whose interest has not yet been correctly aroused. As a life-long bachelor you should sympathize.'

'But, dammit, I . . .'

'Valparaiso does not count, Peregrine.'

'Hell!' said the admiral, turning a deeper shade of tortoise.

'And if Mr Gillon will only feed himself properly as well as Nur Jehan,' Georgina went on unruffled, 'I see no reason why they should not be a great credit to the village. Nur Jehan is a more dignified investment than tomatoes under glass.'

'What sort of mount is he?' I asked, for everyone seemed to be hypnotized into treating the Arab as if he were a prize buck rabbit.

'Being ridden,' Georgina explained, 'is one of the many duties, Charles, which Nur Jehan does not greatly enjoy. And he refuses to be ridden by a woman at all.'

I thought that most improbable – the sort of romantic nonsense which appeals to the unscientific. But who was I to argue with Aunt Georgina on a matter of horses? I had been a horseman at the age of seventeen. The Hungarian branch of the family had seen to that. Since then I had merely used horses whenever they were available and the most convenient method of transport.

'His former owner found no difficulty,' said the vicar mildly, 'nor have I.'

'Because you let him go where he likes at the pace he wants to,' Georgina answered.

I could see that nothing, not even living on porridge – if that were true – was going to separate Matthew Gillon from Nur Jehan. He not only adored the stallion, but had a reasonable and innocent hope of future profit.

'And eventually, Peregrine,' Georgina went on, 'the vicar will have to employ a groom. Benita cannot be expected to come down here just to muck out the stable for him.'

'There's profit in that, too,' I said, remembering Jim Melton and the 'earse.

Cunobel glared at me; but before he had time to point out that, dammit, it wouldn't pay for the straw, Benita Gillon joined us in the kitchen. I had been prepared for my own idea of a female commercial artist and I expected, I think, that she would either muck out the stable in garments altogether too colourful for the job, or else would consider that the rescue of father justified a deal of unnecessary dirt. But I could see no London at all about her, except the fashionably lank fair hair which framed her delicately tanned face. She belonged where she was. I could well understand that she took every excuse to return to her village.

We had barely time for a few words before Aunt Georgina called the admiral and myself to attention and dismissed us. She had intended, I suspect, to parade Benita a couple of hours later when all three of them were coming over to dine, and she was not pleased at the girl's arrival direct from the stable. She was quite wrong there. Benita grew deliciously out of her heavy wellington boots like a graceful young tree from a pot.

The comfort of the admiral and his guests was assured by Frank – naturally a naval production too. He was cook, butler, valet, and intelligence staff. Women were permitted aboard for laundry and floor-scrubbing, for the making of pies, jams, pickles, and larder-stocking in general, which Frank insisted was their work. What he really wanted from them was more intimate village gossip than could be obtained in the pub.

When we came back I saw Frank whispering confidentially to his employer.

'Of course he hasn't, boy!' Cunobel shouted – it was his habit to address anyone under sixty as 'boy' – 'What would he have a dinner jacket for? Wouldn't want a boiled shirt for watching squirrels, eh?'

'Badgers,' I corrected him, not being sure whether he knew that the Hernsholt country was a most improbable haunt of the red squirrel.

'Badgers or rats,' he said oddly, 'all one! He's an old fool, that boy! When we're alone I have to dress for dinner like one of those blazing idiots in the jungle whom Benita draws for the sherry people. And lousy sherry it is! Pah! Knows very well I don't dress when there are guests! Thinks I can't move with the times!'

The dinner went very well, Georgina being on her Court-of-Franz-Joseph behaviour and the admiral and I having primed ourselves to a point of reasonable geniality before the arrival of the guests. Benita was extremely civil, insisting that she had heard so much about me from my aunt and had read my book on the squirrel. She had, too – for she told me that my description of the use of the tail in the gliding jump from branch to branch was misleading.

'Benita, my dear, Mr Dennim is an authority,' said her father.

Her glance at me was delightful. It suggested, while preserving a proper demureness, that we were two professionals and must be patient with the unseemly interruptions of amateurs.

'This is what happens . . .' she said.

She borrowed a pencil from the admiral and an envelope from me. With a dozen swift strokes she caught the feathering of the hair and the angle of tail to body. I agreed at once that she was right and that I had very badly described what I had seen.

To describe Benita herself is even harder. Her true interest, so far as I can explain it, was a sort of sensual geography. She adored her own countryside, upland and valley, whatever the weather. If one imagines a tall fairy or wood nymph – not her appearance, but what would go on in her mind if she existed – then one comes somewhere near Benita.

I do not mean that she was a sort of Rima. Far from it. She was not at all a child of nature. She would have been pretty quickly bored watching squirrels. But if squirrel-watching had been a traditional hobby in the Cotswolds, she would have known all about the people who did it, why they did it, and where.

Another example. One might almost call her a trained observer of grass. This undoubtedly started from the pleasure of a young and rather lonely child in feeling the soft Cotswold turf under foot, in watching the life of the valleys through the thin, waving stems on the edge of the escarpment. But it led her on to know the whole range of the grasses and the tastes of sheep and cattle.

And now I find myself describing a collector of scraps of useless information. That isn't right either. And so I return to my romantic conception of her as a nymph – an entity carrying the collective soul of four square miles of country. I am told that this is all very pretty but that I do not understand parsons' daughters. All the same, I cannot imagine what induced her to become a commercial artist in London. There was never the slightest chance of her becoming, as Georgina said, a mamby pamby old maid.

During the days which I spent cossetted by the admiral and his Frank I naturally saw a good deal of Benita, and recovered other memories of youth in the amateur schooling of Nur Jehan. I refused to consider the future at all. If the tiger had trusted to that speed of attack which had been so nearly successful at the cottage, he would have got me.

I do not say that I would have welcomed such an end; but I was very well aware that the loneliness of death would make less difference to me than to most of my fellows. The little world into which I had fallen was so superficially pleasant, so real to its inhabitants and yet so very unattainable by me. The remoteness which I felt was not wholly due to the twenty years between myself and Benita. I saw them all as beloved actors upon a stage which I, the single spectator in the vast, lonely auditorium, could never approach. I might have been a cripple. I suppose that in a way I was.

Aunt Georgina seemed in no hurry to return to our suburb. She was just as exasperated as Cunobel by the incompetence of the Gillons in dealing with so valuable and unexpected a legacy as Nur Jehan. On the other hand, she flatly refused to persuade the vicar to get rid of him. Dear Peregrine had appealed to her to come and make sense of the situation, and sense she was going to make even if it meant that she was housekeeper and head groom.

Sitting one evening with the admiral and myself at the companionable hour of the aperitif, she firmly pointed out that the Church in ampler days had expected the Vicar of Chipping Marton to keep a horse and carriage and had provided him with a stable and a five-acre meadow. It was absurd to be content with using one as a hen house and with raising and selling a single crop of hay from the other.

'But the wretched animal won't stay in the stable except at night, Georgi!' Cunobel protested.

'Naturally he will not. The place still smells of chickens. We shall all take our meals there for a week, Peregrine, if we can attract him back in no other way. Nur Jehan is worth a little trouble. He is becoming known.'

'Great Blood and Bones, he's a joke from Badminton to Banbury!'

'I have a very good mind to show him at the Bath and West.'

I ascribed this astonishing assertion to the influence of the admiral's old Madeira. It was his insidious habit to compliment her on her palate. The old dear tried to surround her with an illusion that time had stood still since 1912. And he could do it. Although his means were limited, his possessions, accumulated during so many years of high command, were luxurious. The study in which we were sitting could have been that of a Governor-General.

'He'll make you ridiculous, Georgi! He'll slide you off over his tail and then go and sit in the President's box!'

'But they want to see him.'

'Who told you that?'

'One of the patrons of the Bath and West, Peregrine.'

'Which of 'em? I'll get him handed such a rocket!'

'He didn't tell me his name, now I come to think of it. A big, dark man. Not out of his forties, I'd say, but very grey and rides all of fourteen stone. He asked me if I was Mrs von Dennim. God knows where he got the *von*! Charles has never used it since he settled in England, and my husband never did. Most delightful easy manners he had! I must have met him somewhere before.'

'Can you remember where?' I asked.

'Funny you should say that, Charles! I've been racking my brains. I've seen his face somewhere. Or a brother, perhaps.'

'Shopping? Or the riding school? Or in our street?'

'Somewhere like that. But it's just a resemblance. I'm sure it wasn't really him.'

'I think I know the chap you mean, Aunt Georgie,' I went on, for I had to. 'He must have gone white. Didn't he have dark hair and prominent eyebrows?'

'At home?' she replied, rather puzzled. 'Yes. Perhaps. But you know how one person reminds you of another.'

'Where was it that he came up to you and started talking?'

'Up above Didmarton, Charles, when I was leading Nur Jehan.'

The admiral had put down his glass and was simmering in his chair. He had even fiercer eyebrows than the false ones worn on occasion by this delightful patron of the Bath and West. My aunt, who had gone a little pale, for once looked at him more in appeal than command.

'I won't!' Cunobel shouted. 'It's obvious why the boy is asking questions. Damn silly this silence, I call it! Blast!'

'My dear Charles,' said my aunt, recovering her usual composure, 'the Dennims have always had an exasperating habit of protecting their womenfolk, and we all know very well that when you choose to carry on like a lot of knight errants polishing their boots in a heavy silence there is nothing whatever we can do about it. I will leave it at that, merely saying that I have not for one moment believed in your squirrels.'

I pretended to misunderstand. I pointed out that my observations were generally held to be accurate and my theories interesting though debatable.

'All this beating about the bush!' the admiral thundered. 'You let me deal with this in my own way, Georgi! Damn it, I'm the oldest friend the boy has got, and I could tell you all about his type when I was a snotty! Your aunt means that she knows the bomb was meant for you, and that's why you went off to your Warren!'

Quite absurd, I said. If I had thought the bomb was meant for me, I should have stayed at home under police guard instead of exposing myself in the country. And anyway what earthly motive could there be?

'Both of us know the motive as well as you do.'

'Peregrine!' my aunt appealed.

'I will *not* shut up, Georgi. Never heard anything like it in my life! All this devotion to each other and never going near the facts! Sacred Teeth, boy, I've had the girl in tears!'

Georgina in tears was unthinkable. But I still did not know where I was.

'I give you my word of honour, sir, that I do not know any reason for wanting to kill me,' I said. 'And if either of you do, please tell me.'

'Obviously revenge – with a past like yours!'

Georgina took command.

'When you came out of hospital, Charles, I had a talk with your Colonel Parrow. I have never mentioned it to you. We both thought it best that you should forget.'

The unthinkable was true before my eyes. She *was* in tears.

'My fault, Georgi!' Cunobel assured her, his bellow much muted. 'I should have left it alone! But, great Blood and Bones, a von Dennim in the Gestapo! Isn't there a dam' thing those cloak-and-dagger boys won't do? I'd hang the lot of them as war criminals. I saw it all when I was at the Admiralty. Bastards! Take a clean, clever boy and torture him! Damn it, the other side will only shoot him if they catch him, and honour him too! Dirty, lousy tricks they call Intelligence! You've a right to order a man to die, but you've no right to do that to him.'

The admiral's storm of sincerity was effective. I cannot analyse what had been going on in my mind. I know that I had been on the point of walking out of that unbearable house which had exposed my shame. But this protest of an honourable fighting man that the damage you did to the enemy could never excuse the damage done to the individual soul was, though eccentric for these days, extraordinarily comforting.

Oddly enough, my first impulse was to defend my service. It was Hitler's fault, not theirs, that I had landed in the Gestapo.

'There was a right,' I said. 'Perhaps not in former wars, but in the last war when the whole of our Christian civilization was at stake there was no limit to what could be asked. We sold ourselves to the devil for the sake of the faith, and it depends on the God which is within us whether we have to keep the bargain for ever. And no one can help.'

As soon as I had said that, I felt it was far too dramatic and in my case untrue. I apologized to Georgina.

'How much did Ian tell you?' I asked.

'Your precious Ian,' she answered indignantly, 'told me as little as he possibly could. And he wouldn't have said that much if I hadn't made him tell me why you refused your decoration. I also spoke a year later to the Olga Coronel whom you rescued.'

'Did you manage to convince her that I wasn't all I seemed?'

This question, which I may have put bitterly, at once restored dear Georgina to her proper form.

'Charles, you are extraordinarily stupid in all questions of women,' she declared. 'Do you really suppose that after five minutes with you she, one of the most quick and intelligent creatures I have ever come across, did not know the difference between a selfless agent risking his life under British orders and a Gestapo officer corrupt enough to take a bribe?'

She told me all that Olga Coronel had said about me; it was certainly polite. Apparently she had come over from Belgium specially to find and thank me on behalf of Catherine Dessayes and herself. But Georgina and the psychiatrists thought we had better not meet. I can't say whether they were right or wrong. I do not know – mercifully – how much trouble I had given them.

'The trouble with you, boy,' said Cunobel, 'is that because you're not friends with yourself you think nobody else can be.'

I admitted to myself that there was an inevitable element of truth in that. In the recent agitated days I had received astonishing kindness from people who had little means of judging me beyond my face. Charles Dennim couldn't understand it; but I suppose the young Graf von Dennim of twenty years before would have taken it as a matter of course. Had he trust in his fellow men and women, or sheer conceit?

'Now what have you been up to since that poor postman was killed?' the admiral went on. 'Georgi, you'd better have some more Madeira.'

I gave them the barest facts of the story, playing it as a

straight, personal investigation with practically no risk. I noticed that Cunobel twice refilled Georgina's glass and that she was quite unaware of it.

'I see,' he said at last, with a shadow of a wink to me. 'Well, you've done very well, and we'll just set the police on now to establish his identity. Georgi, this has all been a great shock to you. Would you like to lie down a little before you go home?'

I never admired my dear aunt so much as at that moment. She rose stiffly to her feet with concentrated, masculine dignity.

'I promised his mother I would look after him and I will,' she said.

'I never knew you had seen her again after 1914!' the admiral exclaimed, carried away into a slight tactlessness by his surprise.

'It was quite unnecessary, Peregrine, for my sister to be alive in order to make her a promise.'

She swallowed a hiccup and strode dead straight for the door.

'I shall not require a rest of more than ten minutes, and I shall ring for Frank if I want anything,' she said.

When we were satisfied that she had made herself very comfortable in the bedroom next to mine and was sleeping like a child, Cunobel took me through my story again and got the truth. His brain was still as incisive as his speech, and he was right when he claimed to know my type. He made me feel like the captain of a fast cruiser just in from a successful reconnaissance.

'Got the letter from your chap in the Austrian Ministry of Justice?' he asked.

I took it from my wallet and gave it to him, warning him that it was in German.

'And what do you think assistant naval attachés were doing in Vienna before 1914?' he snorted. 'They didn't send 'em there to learn to waltz! Your mother and Georgi found my German as comic as a music-hall turn in those days. But by the time I'd finished two wars I could have written Grand Admiral Raeder's orders for him!'

He put on his glasses and read the letter very slowly twice.

'I thought you were running pretty close to a quibble when

you said you knew no motive for killing you,' he remarked. 'But I see what you mean now. Why you? Why this Sporn, Dickfuss and Weber when there were dozens of other swine as bad? And then you feel sure this fellow wasn't in Buchenwald in your time with or without his eyebrows. Identity unknown. Motive unknown. And if it weren't for you, face unknown too.'

'You think I was right?' I asked with some surprise, for I expected him to take the same view as Ian.

'Right? Of course you were right! I reckon German police are as good as our own, and they don't have to pull their punches either. But he's beaten them. I've got just enough faith in Scotland Yard to believe that they would get him after he killed you – especially with all your Colonel Parrow and I could tell them. But until he does, they are helpless.

'Shall we call 'em in? Well, that's your business, Charles. It's your life. On your description they could certainly root out all his movements in your suburb and establish how he watched you and when. Then, of course, they'll raid Soho and North Kensington because they always do. That won't do 'em much good when the man they want is so respectable he could be a Chief Constable himself. Still, let's assume they do get on to the trail of the right man and are nearly ready to arrest him for the murder of the postman. Don't tell me he wouldn't know they were after him even before they got to the point of asking a few, polite questions! And then where is he? Gone, and waiting to have a crack at you next year!

'I'll tell you what, boy! I think you're wrong when you say he's the sort of chap who might be lunching at my table in the club. He might, so far as his type goes. But in fact he can't be well known in England. Imagine what would happen if he was! There he is, travelling back and forth to Woburn and prowling round your district. Now, if he had a lot of friends, he'd run into one. "Good God, Dick, what's happened to your hair and eyebrows? Changed your barber?" And then it's all over the place in no time. See what I mean?'

He was undoubtedly right. So we had a convincing picture of a man who knew England inside out, but had very few friends here – or, possibly, had not been in the country for so many years that his friends would not easily recognize him.

'Wild guess, Charles!' he went on. 'No good taking it to the police! They want facts, like you scientists, not intelligent conjecture. But one can't win a war that way – not even your private one. All one ever knows of the enemy is conjecture.'

I said that the speed and accuracy of conjecture on the opposite side were more like second sight. I could not understand how he had managed to trace me and begin reconnaissance all within eight days.

'Of course not! A man can't see the wood for the trees when he's sweating with panic. Didn't you say your Isaac Purvis spotted him on the way back from the badgers to the Long Down and that his course would take him past your cottage? Well, where was my letter to you?'

'On the floor of the passage inside the front door.'

'Plenty of time to steam it open with you stuck in a bramble bush!'

I doubted that. He had not plenty of time – five or ten minutes at the most, and those he would have used to prowl around the cottage and make sure it was empty and unwatched, not to steam letters open. It was not in his character to take unnecessary risks.

Otherwise Cunobel was right. The envelope of his letter had looked a bit untidy, which might have aroused my suspicions if I had known his passion for neatness as well as I knew it now. The visitor had simply raised the flap of the envelope with a sharp knife and stuck it up again. If he had made a mess of the job, he would merely have walked off with the letter and I should have been none the wiser.

I asked Cunobel for his frank advice – as my oldest friend, which I really began to feel he was.

'How are your nerves?' he grunted.

I replied that they seemed to be all right, but were evidently affecting my alertness.

'Sleeping well?'

'Sometimes.'

'Ever occurred to you that you're doing a public service?'

I wasn't going to admit that I had once been in a state of drivelling terror while walking along a harmless road, and had comforted myself with that very thought.

'Well, you are. How many other mistakes has he made, besides that poor postman, which we don't know about? It's a bad business, boy. I had a nasty case when I was at the Admiralty. Anonymous letters from a poor devil telling us to make our peace with God because it was his duty to shoot us all. He turned out to be a retired Commander who was crazy as a coot and never showed any other sign of it. Special Branch had the hell of a time running him to earth.

'I remember what the Assistant Commissioner told me. Political assassins – all in the day's work! Criminal lunatics – bothering, but they reckon to pick 'em up! What's a fair nightmare to them is the potential murderer who isn't a political, doesn't mix with criminals, doesn't show any eccentricities. Get at his grievance, and you'll get his identity! But if you haven't a clue to his motive and he's cunning, he'll tie up a considerable force of men on plain guard duties.

'Now, in a case like yours I think Special Branch would try to trap their man. Use a decoy. In fact do just what you are doing. But they'd never allow it without a copper up every tree. Your method is better, but I don't like it. You go on staying with me, Charles. He can't do very much while you're here. Let's sit quiet and see if he makes a mistake!'

That was true enough. At Chipping Marton I was seldom alone, and there was no regularity in my movements. That patron of the Bath and West could only watch. He had little chance of attack without being seen. So long as I remained with the admiral, our game was adjourned for refreshments and I could rest.

But rest is in the mind. There was no feeling it. And this was the more exasperating because I knew that for the first time in twenty years I had all the ingredients of happiness. There was a new, dear warmth between Georgina and myself. There was the training of Nur Jehan. There was my delight in the child, Benita – a desolate delight, for I had to emphasize to myself that she was, compared to a man of forty-three, a child. And

all this ruined because I could not move without a degrading
.22 pistol in my pocket!

Benita had little interest in horses. She could ride, of course.
The local Pony Club had seen to that before she was twelve –
leaving her at the same time with a lasting dislike of the
revivalist religion of the horse and its female pastors. Aunt
Georgina, with her matter-of-fact nineteenth-century attitude,
had been an exception. Georgina shrugged her shoulders at
enthusiasm and simply laid down the law that a person of sense
should know exactly what was going on in his or her stables
just as the modern car driver ought to (but doesn't) know
enough to give precise orders to his garage.

So in the country Benita walked. In London, I gathered,
never. I could not avoid these casual strolls without inexplicable
surliness, and I did not want to. But she very soon spotted my
preference for the open, wind-swept tops of the Cotswolds.

She put down my manner to a curious life and a dangerous
war. Georgina had told her that much. Whether she thought
I needed an exorcist or a psychiatrist I was not sure, and I
don't think she was.

One afternoon she said to me quietly:

'There is nothing behind you, Charles.'

I had looked back twice when passing along the bottom of
a dry valley. The steep sides were clothed with patches of gorse,
intersected by runways of silent turf. It was easy to come down
from the top in short rushes quite unseen, until the range had
closed to ten yards and that intent, dark face was smiling at
my back. What went on ahead of me I did not care. The birds
would give me warning.

I apologized for my restlessness.

'But you look as if you really expected something,' she
said.

'A naturalist always does. The watcher begins to resemble
the watched.'

'Are animals afraid all the time?'

I answered that I did not think so – not in our sense of the
word anyway – but that fear was never far from the surface,
was acceptable and might even be enjoyable. Everything which

preserves must in theory be enjoyable: mating, the satisfaction of hunger and the feeding of the young. A hare, for example, obviously triumphs in a narrow escape; you can see self-confidence in the easy gallop. Extreme danger is pleasurable to a few soldiers – even civilized, sensitive soldiers. And aren't there young idiots in America who drive cars at each other down the centre of the road to see who will get out of the way first?

'All the time, all around us,' I said, 'Death is making his reconnaissance.'

'But it's life which you are afraid of,' Benita replied.

'Because I look behind me?' I laughed.

She accepted that as just an unconscious gesture. I behaved as if I were haunted, she said, only because I was continually looking back into my life instead of forward. There was enough truth in the accusation for me to accept it without awkwardness.

But God knew the haunting was real enough! I had always the impression that I was being watched, though I now believe that at the moment I was not. Physically, that is. Death was at his headquarters, collecting the intelligence reports.

Only Benita saw anything wrong with me. Her father did not. There was no reason why he should. The link between us – all the link I was admitting – was Nur Jehan. Since he fought Georgina and Benita, and Gillon when on his back was too indulgent, only I could begin to school him.

It was never fair to call the vicar unpractical. What he lacked was capital, not common sense. He was a most lovable man, unaffected, fully able to hold the respect of his parishioners outside the church and their attention within it. His only worry – a severe worry – was Chipping Marton Vicarage, which he could not even keep in proper repair. He was rightly determined that at least the garden should bring in an income to pay for the house.

'My dear Dennim,' he said to me once, 'you are a man of the world. You would probably agree that I should be fully justified in turning the vicarage into a guest-house or in using my leisure, such as it is, to practise some harmless form of commerce or home industry.'

I did not agree – and since I knew that he didn't either I said so.

'The limit of the permissible,' he went on. 'Yes, one soon arrives at it. Two hundred years ago the vicar of Chipping Marton worked the land and fed his family. We clergy of today have not the time and probably not the skill. Yet to produce, to make grow, to create – that much I feel is allowable to a servant of the Creator. I have given my spare time to specialities with some success. You will find *Gloxinia Rev. Matthew Gillon* in most nurserymen's catalogues, though I doubt if I made fifty pounds out of it. I grew tomatoes and strawberries for seed. Admiral Cunobel was unconvinced, but I was able materially to assist Benita in London until it appeared that the varieties which had been recommended to me were very subject to disease. I feel that Nur Jehan is in that category of innocent creation which I permit myself. My conscience insists that to keep so beautiful an animal at stud is a valuable service to the community.'

The real trouble was that Gillon never saw or couldn't afford to see that capital was essential to consolidate the results of his industry. But, granted a run of luck, it might not have been. The admiral, though ribald, had never discouraged his parson until the arrival of Nur Jehan. At least strawberries and tomatoes could not career down the village street looking for affection, or roll luxuriously in an angry neighbour's uncut hay.

Matthew Gillon was unnecessarily grateful and always very conscious that I might be sacrificing my interests to his affairs. He made a point of collecting nature notes from his parishioners in case they might be of use to me, and he pressed his daughter, who was very properly inarticulate about everything she really valued, to show me the secret places of her childhood.

Benita, however, rather resented my profession since she ascribed to it the sudden fits of distraction which interrupted conversation. In any case she wasn't interested in causes, only in effects. If you can catch with your pencil the essential mechanics of a bird's wing and the subtle change of shading which marks on an open down the transition from one grass to another, mere words are dull and the microscope irrelevant.

She did sometimes condescend to pass on facts in the sort of voice which you would expect from a nymph surprised by a zoologist in dark glasses. One afternoon when her father and I were mucking out the stable and she was soaping leather, she remarked:

'There are squirrels in the Wen Acre Plantation if you want to watch them.'

The Plantation was of mixed conifers and beech at the head of the dry valley where Benita and I had walked – an early and most successful experiment of the Forestry Commission which belonged to its countryside as honestly as any other Cotswold wood. It deserved to lose its artificial name and be called the Wen Acre Hanger.

'How blind we are!' Gillon exclaimed. 'I have driven along that road once a week for eight years.'

I suggested that he was not likely to see squirrels from a car when passing along the upper end of the Plantation.

'And anyway, Daddy,' Benita added, 'they weren't there last summer.'

'Weren't they indeed? Well, the little imps have found the perfect home. Bless me, I haven't seen a red squirrel since before the war! I shall certainly stop when I pass tomorrow.'

When I saw him the following evening he was full of triumph and humility. He had started early for the weekly visit to a bed-ridden old shepherd which took him past the top of the Plantation, and had spent an hour wandering under the trees.

'Three I saw for certain,' he announced, 'and I believe there were four. I thought I had found the drey, too, though on the way home I had to admit to myself that it was an old magpie's nest.'

He told us how he had stayed perfectly still for twenty minutes – the amateur always feels that anything over ten is a marvel of patience – and that one of the squirrels had actually come close to his feet, trustful as a grey squirrel in a park.

'I ventured greatly,' he went on. 'I offered a piece of biscuit. It took it in its paws and ate it, looking at me all the time. I – I was amazed! And flattered! So you feel, Dennim, that I was justified?'

'Oh, Daddy, it was somebody's pet!' said Benita.

It must, of course, have been a squirrel brought up by human hands and then turned loose. But I did not want to spoil the vicar's vision of himself as a humble disciple of St Francis. In any case he had every right to pride himself on moving cautiously and giving an impression of saintly harmlessness. It does not take long for a tame animal to become as wild as its companions.

I could not resist going up to have a look at the squirrels myself. I went alone, for it would have been impossible to explain to Benita why I took such care to avoid cover till I knew it was empty. There were four of them, fine little beasts with rather darker tails than usual.

I could not find the two dreys any more than the vicar. Normally that would have been a challenge and I should have spent a couple of weeks on verifying what the family life of the two pairs really was. But I was impatient. My time was fully taken up, Nur Jehan had just begun to answer his helm, as the admiral put it, by pressure of legs alone.

I saw little of him except at dinner, for his local dictatorship extended beyond his own village and vicar and he kept himself busy with all the usual bumbling committees, where he was dreaded for his outspokenness but indispensable. He considered it a duty of hospitality to preserve his guests from the teas and luncheons which accompanied these activities, so that I was surprised when he told me that I had been specially included in an invitation from General Sir Thomas Pamellor.

'Who is he?' I asked.

'The county's prize pongo,' said the admiral. 'Lives just the other side of Cirencester. But he'll give you the best lunch outside London if you can stand him.'

'What's the matter with him?'

'Matter with him is that he's a bore, boy! Good God, when Thomas retired they had to call in extra police to control the celebrations in Whitehall! It had got so bad that if you had a position of any responsibility in this country you couldn't talk to a visiting Frenchman without Thomas dropping in beforehand to tell you what you oughtn't to say. Hell's Bells, if there's anything we and the French don't know about each other after a thousand years of fun and games, that ass Thomas is the last person to spot it! But his cook, boy! Mustn't miss that! A pity we can't take Frank with us. He might pick up a hint or two.'

General Sir Thomas Pamellor at once reminded me of a fine, freshly caught shrimp. Not that he was small, but he sprouted hair at odd angles from eyebrows and moustache, and his colouring was exactly the right mixture of sand and grey. Lady Pamellor was a slightly smaller shrimp, but cooked. She was bright pink and had a good deal of pink in her dress. She gazed at her still living companion with admiration. There was not much else she could do, for Sir Thomas never stopped giving us extracts from his unwritten memoirs throughout six courses.

'Frankly I never knew a Frenchman I couldn't get on with,' said Pamellor. 'I was only a colonel then, but whenever and wherever there was trouble with the French Churchill gave the same order: turn Pamellor loose on 'em!'

'Very right!' the admiral agreed naughtily. 'You're the last person they would suspect of playing a deep game.'

'Exactly, Cunobel! A simple soldier and simple liaison. You can't have too much of it. Now then, *mon vieux*, I used to say, here's British policy! And I'd tell him. Here's French policy! And I'd tell him that, too. Then all we had to do was to go our own way and make the thing work.'

'He speaks such *very* beautiful French,' said Lady Pamellor, making her sole contribution to the conversation.

And on he went.

'Just tell me what you want, I said to de Gaulle, and I'll see that Churchill falls in with it. So far as he can, of course, so far as he can! Our own army, that was the trouble. I remember one of our very high commanders. I won't mention his name. "Any more from you," I said, "and I'll send a signal straight to the Cabinet."'

'And did you?' Cunobel asked.

'God bless my soul, yes! I was always sending signals direct to the Cabinet. I remember a major of the Deuxième Bureau, when I was in Paris after the war, warning me that they had copies of all of them.'

'Broke your cipher, you mean?'

The admiral choked, and did his best to pretend that a truffle had gone the wrong way.

'Good Lord, no! My little secretary had been pinching the *en clair* drafts from the wastepaper basket. "Never mind!" I said to the major. "There's nothing I tell my government that I am not prepared to tell yours." A pity that I hadn't more influence on policy! I could have made us just a band of brothers.'

When Lady Pamellor had swum delicately off and hidden herself beneath the rocks of the drawing room, Sir Thomas pressed cigars upon us and one of the finest brandies I have ever tasted. I can well imagine the French putting out a legend that they found him useful.

'I hear you've been in a spot of trouble, Dennim,' he said.

I instantly joined the odd thousand Europeans who must have thought it wise to impress Sir Thomas with their sincerity.

'Trouble?' I asked, puzzled. 'No.'

'Bomb, eh?'

'Where did you hear that?'

'Shall we say I read it in the paper?' replied the general with heavy diplomacy.

Cunobel was magnificent.

'Dam' Cypriots!' he exclaimed. 'Didn't leave that kind of thing to the army when I was a boy! Sent a cruiser, gave 'em a party and showed 'em over the gun turrets!'

'Cypriots?' Sir Thomas asked. 'They didn't tell me you had been in Cyprus.'

'I've been in a lot of places, my dear general,' I said mysteriously. 'Now which particular *they* are you referring to?'

He was a little taken aback. He had evidently thought this was going to be a straightforward job where the renowned Pamellor frankness would be effective.

'There's no reason why I shouldn't tell you,' he said. 'I've been directly approached by French police. They want to know if you can give any description at all of the man who sent the bomb.'

'No, I can't,' I answered. 'And, anyway, Scotland Yard knows all I know. But how did the Sûreté find out that I was staying somewhere near you?'

'I don't know. I suppose Scotland Yard told them that much but wouldn't tell them any more. Hidebound! I could recommend them half a dozen first-rate fellows who would improve liaison with the Sûreté out of recognition. But there it is! They are up against British mistrust all the time! So what more natural than to appeal to me? Our good friend Pamellor, somebody says, hides himself in his little *gentilhommière* at a few kilometres from Chipping Marton. *Lui, il fera notre affaire!*'

'I do wish I could help a bit more,' I said heartily. 'But, to tell you the honest truth, I am not even sure that the bomb which killed our postman was meant for me.'

'I may pass that on, Dennim?'

'Of course. Was the inquiry from Paris?'

'From the very top. But it's quite likely they were passing on an unofficial inquiry from one of the departments. We old comrades of the Resistance, we serve each other without questions.'

We retired to the drawing-room for coffee, where the admiral discussed with Lady Pamellor some fussy problem of the Girl Guides and the Grammar School, while I was lectured by Sir Thomas on the blindness of the Foreign Office. When at last we got away, Cunobel's driving expressed his feelings. He roared down a mile of straight, screeched round two corners and stopped.

'What do you make of it, Charles?'

I said that it seemed incredible but that I was sure the inquiry really had come to Sir Thomas from France.

'You don't think Pongo is after you himself?'

'Not enough sense.'

'Or friend of Pongo?'

'That's possible. Likely, even. I can imagine him poring over the map to see who he knows or ever has known within riding distance of Chipping Marton. But I don't think he'd risk writing to Sir Thomas himself or calling on him. Not yet. And why should he when he can get some French official to do it for him?'

'But damn it, the man we want is English!'

'If he is, he has some very influential friends in France.'

We sat there in the car trying to think it out, but got no further than the obvious fact that the tiger wanted to know whether I could or could not recognize him. That proved he had not the least suspicion that I had examined him at leisure; but he could not be sure how much I had seen from my perch in the alder. In fact the action on the edge of the badger fortress had been too quick and darkness too far advanced for me to make out anything more than a lump of darkness detaching itself in five quick strides.

The admiral drove on along the top of the Cotswolds while I sat beside him watching that soft sweep of windy country and wondering how and with what gentlemanly excuse the tiger would propose to spring. He was planning to walk straight up to me, perhaps with a cheerful good evening. But where? What lonely spot would allow him to play with his victim, kill and retreat unnoticed? Since few of my movements were regular or easily to be anticipated, how was he to ensure my unsuspecting presence on the ground he had reconnoitred and chosen? Telephone? False message? But I would suspect any and every appointment which might be with death.

What had been his movements since meeting Georgina and confirming that we were both likely to be at Chipping Marton for some time? He might have gone over to France and back several times. He might have been in the Wen Acre Plantation when the instinct of the hunted told me he was thinking of me and made me look again and again behind me.

France ... the Plantation ... and then I saw it. The tails of the squirrels! I had noticed the darker red of the tails and accepted it as a mildly interesting sport of colour in the native English breed. But they weren't English. They were French squirrels. That was why neither Gillon nor I could find the dreys. That accounted for his St Francis act. Three bagged wild, and one from a pet dealer!

And how beautifully simple! The price of my death in Wen Acre Plantation was four red squirrels flown over from France and let loose in a perfectly natural home. A gamble, of course. I might not hear of them. I might pay little attention to them. But if I did, and made a point of watching them, what an opportunity! And he had lost it just because of the one slip of putting France into my head.

I kept this discovery to myself, for I was not yet sure what use I could make of it. I was far from the mood of friendlessness and distrust which had first led me to tackle the whole business alone; but there was no direct help which I could ask. To expose Georgina, the Vicarage and Cunobel to anxiety and possible danger was unthinkable. Tying out the goat when the result mattered only to himself was allowable. Tying him out when he was a village pet was cruel.

There were other reasons why the Plantation could not be put to use. I was up against the old problem in its clearest form. Picket the Wen Acre with police and we should have no more news of my persistent follower, however well their presence was hidden or disguised. Tempt him by leaving it wide open and I should be hit before I dared shoot. The right policy was to station a first-class shot able to arrest or wound in the second or two after the tiger had made his criminal intention plain. But, assuming the police believed every word of my story – and it was a big assumption – where would they find such a man, willing and able to work patiently day after day with me? Anyway that plan had already failed, even with Ian to help.

No, there was nobody but myself. And I must never accept the tiger's conditions; I must impose my own. Against his superb cunning in approach I must set my own superiority in fieldcraft and the overwhelming advantage of being able to recognize him when he had no suspicion that I could.

Back I was going – and in that I was determined – to what I called the Saxon England, that imitation of forest which was no forest at all. But how? I was having no more of lonely cottages where sleep and food were so dangerous that I could never stage a convincing act of living a normal life.

The admiral's usual evening meal was leisurely and ceremonious, but after lunching with Sir Thomas all we could face was a poached egg and some beer. When we had finished, there were still two hours of soft midsummer daylight. Cunobel settled down on the grey stone terrace with a blueprint of the plumbing in a proposed village hall, for he would never admit to himself that he intended to be idle. I guessed that what he really wanted was to admire his roses in peace, so I strolled down to the Vicarage.

Georgina, alone on the lawn and smoking a cigarette much too fast, was very glad to see me. Her mood resembled that of some kindly cavalry colonel with a nasty hangover; she was dignified, hurt and well aware that she had brought her troubles on herself. We now had the fences of the Glebe meadow in first-class order, so she had taken it upon herself – pooh-poohing the advice of Gillon and Benita – to introduce Nur Jehan to the opposite sex under her personal supervision. The stallion had found his companion charming but annoyingly affectionate. He preferred to talk to Georgina over the gate.

She therefore left him alone. Quarter of an hour later she heard screams for help from the vestry window of the church. Nur Jehan had kicked down the wicket-gate between the meadow and the churchyard. The latch on the church door gave him no trouble at all. Once inside and needing comfort, he was delighted to find a human being; it was the organist, a maiden lady of vaguely artistic leanings and excitable. When her variations on the Wedding March were interrupted by a velvet nose pushed into the back of her neck, she had rocketed off her stool and taken refuge in the vestry.

My aunt, whose first duty was to the valuable mare now loose on the road, had been short and notably profane. By the time she had caught and stabled both horses, and the Vicar and Benita had rescued the organist, there was an interested crowd outside the church. Even Georgina, who had no false modesty, was inhibited from explaining the situation to so large an audience.

'What Nur Jehan needs,' I declared, 'is work. No kitchen. No petting. Hard work.'

'I couldn't agree more, Charles,' she said. 'I do not know how they manage these things in Persia, but it stands to reason that when a horse is surrounded by boundless desert he must be taught to consider the master's tent as home. And how to un-teach him, I frankly do not know.'

It was the word *tent* which triggered my instant and clear reaction.

'I think I will take Nur Jehan over to Buckinghamshire and back,' I said, 'before Matthew Gillon starts to sleep in the stable. Do you suppose you could get his permission?'

'No, Charles. But Benita might.'

'Shall I tackle her or will you?'

My aunt observed me with unnecessary exasperation.

'Benita should return to London,' she said. 'Incompetence makes her very nervous.'

'She ought to be used to her father by now.'

'You can take it that I was referring to Nur Jehan's peculiari-ties, Charles.'

I should have left it at that in former days, and said nothing. But I could no longer fence with Georgina now that I knew with what silent devotion she had endured me.

'I am forty-three,' I said, 'and that's twenty years older than she is.'

'A difference,' replied my aunt, 'which ensures a long widow-hood for Benita, but could make her marriage extremely happy. With my own husband I had only thirteen and a half months and one leave. I may be romantic, but I have always considered it was worth the forty years which followed.'

I kissed her and tried to explain that I only wanted similar happiness for Benita, and that a man of twice her age with an unfortunate past and an adopted country could hardly be ex-pected to give it.

I found Benita in the orchard. The inhabitants of the vicarage all seemed to have gone their own way after so agitated an even-ing. She listened to my proposal and agreed that it would do Nur Jehan a world of good. She gave a very strong impression of resenting his existence. The stallion was certainly taking up too much of her father's time and hers.

Together we visited Matthew Gillon in his study to obtain his consent. He agreed, but very gravely doubted whether his late parishioner's pet could conscientiously be treated as a hack. I had to promise that I would cover no more than twenty miles a day till Nur Jehan was in condition.

I was fortunate in being able to settle all this on the top of a wave of general disgust with poor Nur Jehan. But when I said good night to Georgina, she had had time to think. It occurred to her that I might be off to play the private detective again. I didn't deny it, but assured her that I only wanted to confirm a theory and that it was impossible for the patron of Bath and West to find out about my camping holiday in time to take advantage of it.

I slept on the plan. I believed it would succeed. In any case the risk was no worse than if I returned to town. I could not go on indefinitely with real or pretended holidays. I had to carry on my daily London life, pressed in crowds, moving by predictable routes, standing on Underground platforms, taking extreme precautions with my food. This journey with Nur Jehan was safer – tempting to my assassin, yet so natural as to be above suspicion.

Admiral Cunobel, when I tackled him after breakfast, agreed. My story of the French squirrels led him to underrate my opponent. The lovely simplicity of the tiger's plan, which frankly terrified me, did not impress him so much as the insignificant mistakes. It was the legal aspects of my counter-attack which bothered him most.

'There's my evidence,' he said, 'and Colonel Parrow's. Worth a lot, of course, but all hearsay! We have it from you, and you only. Look at it this way, boy! He's a bloody murderer, but we know he is a person ordinarily above suspicion. Suppose you kill him. Suppose there is nothing at all to connect him with the Gestapo executions and not quite enough to convict him of blowing up the postman, where are you then?'

I promised Cunobel that I did not intend to kill him if I could possibly avoid it. All I wanted was identity and motive. I foresaw that I might have to get them at the point of a pistol. But the police could do the rest.

'That pop-gun of yours – I don't like it. Won't knock a man down,' he said. 'I'll let you into a secret. Very wrong. Against the Law. But I couldn't bring myself to get rid of my souvenirs. I keep 'em well locked up, of course, and I've got a fire-arms certificate, but it doesn't cover all the lot.'

He took me into his bedroom, and with the air of a small boy exhibiting his treasures unlocked a cupboard at the back of his built-in wardrobe. There were a German dirk, a broken lance-head, a Japanese sword and a collection of fire-arms – some amateur and suggesting far-off encounters with Arab slave-traders and Malay pirates, some so modern and professional that he was certainly liable to that heavy fine of which Ian had warned me.

'That's what you want,' he said, handing me a .45 revolver.

But it wasn't. I saw the familiar wooden holster of a German Mauser. It was a weapon which I had carried in early days as a forester, for I could afford nothing better. When I was accustomed to it, I wanted nothing better. The holster formed a butt for the long-barrelled automatic, and using the weapon as a rifle – as I always did – it was dead accurate at a hundred yards.

I took it down and inspected it. Like everything else which belonged to Cunobel, the Mauser was in bright, naval condition.

'It can jam,' I said, caressing it, 'and it drills instead of knocking down, but I have a feeling I am more confident over sights than he is.'

I sounded to myself unreal, as if I were diffidently recommending some favourite bar which I had known in youth.

'What? That one?' the admiral asked surprised. 'I got it off a submarine commander in the first war. Don't suppose it's ever been used!'

'But have you any ammo? I'll want at least twenty rounds before I can be sure how she throws.'

'Well, they can't trace the number,' he grumbled with some satisfaction, 'if – er – well, if it was found lying about. I think I might risk it. It would be useful on rabbits, eh? I can't afford a good .22 rifle with my pension, eh? I'll go up to London tomorrow and get you a couple of boxes from old friends at the Admiralty. When will you start?'

'Pammellor's letter should be in Paris tomorrow. I don't think our friend will be content with the usual speed of French official communications. He will know the answer – probably verbally – in three or four days more. His next move is to close in boldly. You may find him calling on you to propose a prize for the best French essay in the Grammar School.'

'Damn his impudence!' the admiral exclaimed. 'But he doesn't need to. We know the fellow is well up in the horsy world. He can find out that Mr Dennim is exercising the Arab stallion without coming nearer than a Bath hotel. He'll be after you at once.'

I did not think so. It would take him time to choose and prepare a base, though he must have one or two possibles lined up already.

'I hope he chooses Gorble again,' I said, 'because then I've got him. I reckon that if I start at the beginning of next week I should be in close contact by the end of it.'

4

THE LONG NIGHT

THE Arab stallion and his rider showed themselves again and again on the bare skyline above the plain of the Severn. The villages where I bought forage and supplies could give news of us, and the farmers from whom I asked permission to camp. Yet all was peace and sun and waving grass. Fear dwindled to a reasonable caution and could not nag me with an image of those dedicated feet pacing behind. No other horseman was glimpsed for an instant across the long ridges of the Cotswolds.

This was Benita's England: the line of uplands which formed a pathway from the Atlantic beaches into the heart of the land. Its naked gentleness saddened me, for beauty which is foreign to the spirit and unattainable creates a loneliness. With the Saxons, creeping up their muddy estuaries into the forest, I had easy sympathy. My heredity was theirs; what they thought a site for a settlement would also be my choice. But here was a glory of my adopted land which did not belong to me. My roots searched over the surface of the rock, unable for the moment to penetrate more deeply.

It was perfect country, however, for my purpose – which was to call up the tiger on to ground of my own choosing. I did not expect him in full daylight. An attack would be most difficult to carry through with the clean certainty of success which he preferred. But dusk and a lonely man should tempt him.

Georgina had supplied me with a list of inns and farms where a horse would be welcome for the night. I did not use them. My evening routine was to camp early in woodland by one of the hidden Cotswold streams and then, having picketed Nur Jehan, to watch the approaches from a tree or high ground. If I saw any doubtful traveller, I stalked and investigated him. When I knew that my position had not been reconnoitred before nightfall I could sleep in peace.

Apart from my careful selection of camp sites too secluded to be easily approached in darkness, I did nothing unexpected. My intentions would be plain to any interested person pricking out my north-easterly route upon the inch ordnance map. I was keeping off the metalled roads as far as possible and obviously aiming for the short turf and empty fields around the sources of Churn and Windrush. After that I might turn back to Chipping Marton or go on – as I intended – through Banbury and Brackley to the Long Down and the patch of Midland country already familiar to the tiger.

I sent a postcard every day to comfort Matthew Gillon, who was still uneasy at the thought that Nur Jehan was being treated as a real horse. The stallion was amenable to any plan. He considered me, I think, a fellow male and playmate – a better one than the vicar's pigs which could never get out of their sty or the village children who ran away or women whose proper place was in the kitchen tent. If I also wished to sit on his back, that was a matter which could easily be arranged to the satisfaction of two gentlemen. Obedience, he had none; good will, plenty. He was accustomed to single rein and unjointed snaffle, and neither his former owner nor the vicar had ever ridden him up to that.

Too many memories of youth crowded in for my safety. Half of me joyously dropped twenty years and concentrated on schooling this sensitive and lovely aristocrat who was anxious as a boy on a football field to do the right thing if only someone would explain the game. The other half – the old goat which had no use for memories but wanted to live – found Nur Jehan an embarrassment. It was difficult to give enough attention to my own security while trying to make chocolate-and-cream playfulness understand the language of the legs.

He had to carry a light sleeping bag and ground sheet as well as his own blanket, and until he was in condition I seldom gave him my own weight as well. We mostly marched in the morning and devoted an hour in the afternoon to education. As a packhorse he was reliable. He followed to heel like a well-trained dog, occasionally amusing himself by butting me from behind when I least expected it.

On my way I answered questions freely, saying that I was going through Banbury to Hernsholt where I had a cottage and would stay a few nights. So it was simple to pick up my trail. I was covering only some twenty miles a day; anyone could keep close contact with me by taking an innocent evening's run in a car and stopping for a drink in villages which I had passed. I reckoned that if the dark rider was again going to make use of Fred Gorble he should already have made his arrangements and left his pugmark in the neighbourhood.

On the sixth night I camped between Brackley and Buckingham, and next day rode across country to call on Jim Melton, making a wide circuit round Hernsholt for I did not wish Ian Parrow to hear of my presence. My respectful affection for him was unchanged, and arguments were to be avoided. I no longer felt the false affinity to Jim as one outcast to another – my lonely sense of being eternally dirtied was much less after the warmth of Chipping Marton and the revelation that Georgina had always known my secret – but as a discreet ally Jim was a man after my own heart.

Mrs Melton was at home. So were her two daughters who ought to have been at school. I gathered that they were under convenient suspicion of developing mumps. Jim had a magnificent crop of early new potatoes and needed the family labour for a couple of days.

Half an hour after my arrival he drove up in the hearse with a load of cut-price sacks and boxes. He was amazed to find Nur Jehan in his kitchen and on excellent terms with everyone – except the jackdaw who was outside and cursing. Mrs Melton had considered it natural that the stallion should try to follow me into the house, again confirming my suspicion that she was half or altogether a gipsy.

The dark gentleman had not been seen and had made no approach to Fred Gorble. Mrs Melton was sure of that. Ever since the evening when she had called on Gorble and muddled him with messages from a fictitious and mysterious lady whom the gentleman was supposed to be secretly visiting, she had been accepted as Gorble's adviser in the whole tricky and possibly profitable business.

The tiger had put through his telephone call at the appointed time, and had been informed by two simple No's that there had been no inquiries about his movements and that I had left the Warren. Encouraged by these replies, he had asked two more questions and again given a date and time when he would telephone for the answers. Meanwhile Gorble had received through the post an envelope with twenty much-used pound notes in it. Damned if Mrs Melton hadn't managed to get hold of five of them!

The two new questions were: what had I been doing at Hernsholt and who was my companion? The first was easy to answer. Everyone knew that I had been watching badgers. The second question was harder, for at the cottage I had been alone. Gorble asked Mrs Melton to get the required information.

Neither she nor Jim knew anything about my attempt to trap the dark gentleman at the badger sett. So far as they were aware, I never had any companion; but, if I did, it could only be Colonel Parrow. Mrs Melton knew that there was something mysterious in my relations with Ian, so she had not answered the truth. She informed Gorble triumphantly:

'Another perfesser!'

She couldn't have done better. That would dispel the tiger's suspicions that the goat had been deliberately tied out.

She gave me two other bits of information which fitted neatly into what I already knew. The first call had come from Bath. Fred Gorble heard the operator say: 'You're through, Bath.' The second came from somewhere abroad through the continental exchange.

So much for tampering with the enemy's sources of intelligence. But all I had really gained was the certainty that he had no intention of returning to Fred Gorble and had discovered some surer base for attack.

Now that I knew it, it stood to reason. Why go to the trouble of planting these squirrels unless he had decided where to stay and how to take advantage of them? And whatever base he had arranged for murder in the Wen Acre Plantation would serve for murder anywhere else in the central and southern Cotswolds. He might be staying under a false name at a Bath or

Bristol hotel. He might be using his true name – playing his distinction and money for all they were worth and spending a magisterial week or two, completely above suspicion, under the roof of some county magnate.

I said good-bye to this delightful and rascally family – who from me would never take a penny – and told them that neither they nor Fred Gorble were ever likely to hear any more of the dark gentleman. As I was about to mount Nur Jehan, Mrs Melton offered to read my hand assuring me that she really did have a gift. I refused. Like most people, I am thoroughly superstitious without believing a word of it. Whether I had a predictable future or not depended on myself, and any foreboding or false confidence could be deadly.

'Well, I'll tell you one thing,' she said. 'The same fate is on the horse and the goat in the same place.'

This was intriguing, for she had picked the symbol of the goat out of my mind and it didn't seem to have occurred to her – unless she was being professionally mysterious – that the symbol was myself.

Under the circumstances I simply could not resist asking more.

'What about the goat and the tiger, Mrs Melton?'

She held my hand for that one, and suddenly turned a little pink as if in genuine anger.

'Tormenting poor dumb animals is a thing I won't 'ave, and I won't look at it,' she said.

I rode off. I did not need Mrs Melton's muddle of telepathy and second sight to tell me that the reckoning would be painful for one or both. I had given the tiger time to prepare his plan. I had shown him my routine. I had convinced him that I was unprotected. On my way home the attack would come.

I felt equal to him on the bare tops and more than his equal in the wooded valleys where I hid my camp. I was uneasy, but the sanctuary of trees in the dusk is no less because the unknown may be behind or beneath them. I believe that for the animals always and for man sometimes fear is only a vivid awareness of one's unity with nature.

What I did not like was riding along the verge of the roads

when it could not be avoided. A passing car and a burst from a tommy-gun seemed altogether too chancy, gangsterish and out of character, but it was a possibility which I had to consider.

Once we may have been in close contact. Soon after dawn on the third day of my journey back from Brackley I was riding Nur Jehan over the uplands not far from the Rollright Stones. Coming down hill to a desolate crossroads which I had to pass I saw a grey car drawn up by the side of the road. Nothing else was in sight or likely for another hour to be in sight but the low stone walls marking out two chess-boards of grass on each side of a little river. There was no simple reason why a car should be parked at that hour commanding the only two roads by which I could come. A single man was in it, slouched down in the driving seat and apparently asleep, but the rising sun was on the windscreen and I could not see his face.

If I hesitated and changed direction I should show prematurely that I was on my guard; if I rode straight ahead I must pass the car at a range of a couple of yards. I compromised by dismounting, unrolling my kit and making a second breakfast. It was a pleasant and natural spot to choose. After half an hour the occupant of the car reversed into the cross road and drove away. Whether he was awakened by the smell of my coffee or exasperated by my leisurely preparation of it I never knew.

From here I could have followed the south-eastern edge of the Cotswolds and returned Nur Jehan to Chipping Marton in a couple of days. It seemed too soon – a blank ending with all to being over again and the initiative out of my hands once more. So we travelled west and spent the third night above Broadway.

On the fourth day I followed the watershed to the south, aiming for Roel Gate. This was all open country, silent except for the jingle of Nur Jehan's bit and the larks which continually sprang up in front of us and hovered singing. On my outward journey I had passed along the edge of it wishing that I had time to stop and devote a couple of days entirely to the schooling of Nur Jehan. I had arbitrarily set myself Jim Melton's cottage as a destination and refused to deviate from the stages.

But now I had all the time in the world – or as much of it as the tiger was inclined to allow me.

The country seemed short of my own special requirements, which were water for Nur Jehan and close cover for me. So I looked through the list of addresses which Georgina had given me, and found a promising spot some three or four miles away, just south of the road from Stow-on-the-Wold to Tewkesbury.

I was welcomed effusively by the hearty lady who owned this immense and probably unproductive farm. Her main interest, to judge by the deep, ripe carpet of dogs around her feet, was the breeding of still more of them. She explained that she was no rider herself – the doggies would be jealous – but that all the Pony Clubs knew of her lovely barn.

I listened with formal courtesy to a flow of reminiscences larded with the names of distinguished horsewomen – few men – who had stayed at her house or camped at the lovely barn. She insisted on showing me the bedrooms and how comfortable they were. I chose the barn rather to her surprise. At last I obtained my dismissal and directions to ride up the hill to a clump of trees just over the horizon.

The huge, empty barn stood among a thick windbreak of beeches. It was desolate and austere, I thought, rather than lovely; but it was dry, with the honey smell of centuries of Cotswold hay. The site was perfect in good weather for horse and man. Spring water splashed into a trough. The silent turf stretched away for a half mile to the north and west.

The clump of trees was altogether too easy to find in darkness; and that I was there could be confirmed from a long way off by a good pair of binoculars or even by a discreet use of the telephone. My usual evening reconnaissance would not therefore be of much value. Yet the more I looked at the place, the more I felt this might be the end. The tiger could purr with satisfaction. After a quiet and quick attack he would have all the rest of the night to get clear of the body. But since I was expecting him, the odds were on the defence – so heavily that I reckoned I could deal with him mercifully. And that was still essential. I could not kill him unless he had a gun in his hand.

Even so, I hoped to be able to talk before deciding what to do with him.

Nur Jehan thought the place a horse's paradise. He was coming on fast. In action over open country or on the verge of a road he was now quick to obey and intelligent. His only fault was in quieter movement – out of school, as it were – when he saw no reason why he should be prevented from light entertainment, such as trying to stamp with his forelegs on silly chickens, or from stopping to eat whatever took his fancy.

About four in the afternoon I was grooming Nur Jehan, who had at last been taught to change from trot to canter with the off fore leading. The stallion was reproachful, for his mouth hurt – he was so unused to discipline that it would have hurt if he had been bitted with a velvet-covered willow-twig – and I was completely absorbed in rewarding him with all the sensual pleasure which curry-comb and brush could give.

I looked up suddenly at the sound of hooves, remembering that the Mauser was under my coat ten good yards away, and observed with relief the arrival of Benita. Under the circumstances my welcome showed more than the usual fatherly warmth. It must have sounded enthusiastic.

'How did you find us?' I asked.

'Well, your last postcard said you would pass one side or the other of Stow-on-the-Wold today. So Georgina asked a friend of hers to put me up for a couple of nights and lend me a pony. Daddy was getting anxious.'

I inquired no further. I was well aware of my aunt's opinion, but I did not agree. I had no intention of letting Benita know what I thought of her and I did my best not to admit it to myself. It was not my business to know which of them had proposed the visit.

'After that it was easy,' Benita went on. 'Georgina's girl-friend telephoned all the other horsy people, and we soon heard you were at the barn. Why don't you stay at the farm and be comfortable?'

'Too many dogs,' I said. 'Nur Jehan and I don't like them.'

It evidently puzzled her that I, who was always looking

around and behind me, should choose to sleep in so lonely a spot.

'You are not expecting anybody?' she asked.

That was too close to the bone. Since I detected a faintly jealous note in her voice, I replied with deliberate vulgarity that men of my age generally preferred luxury hotels to haystacks.

'But you,' she said, 'would be quite likely to choose a gorse bush. What's that under your coat?'

She had caught a glimpse of the Mauser in its holster as I moved my kit to make room for her between the smooth roots of a great beech. I told her that it was a wooden horseman's flask, and ascribed it vaguely to the Carpathians.

'What do you keep in it?'

'Wine. The wood gives a bitter taste. You wouldn't like it.'

She looked disappointed. Some form of hospitality would ease the perceptible tension between us. I offered her whisky and spring water which I mixed in vicar's daughter proportions. I always found it difficult to remember that she was also a commercial artist.

I think it was because her face had that exquisite mixture of liveliness and innocence which belongs to seventeen rather than twenty-three, and is in any case more common among French than English. She had no lack of worldly wisdom. Her tough profession saw to that. She accepted life as it was; but she was rooted so firmly in her beloved countryside that life as it was seemed to her more to be enjoyed than pitied. I don't mean that she was insensitive. She did not think of natural beauty as an escape from humanity. She had no need of escape at all.

'We have talked so much about you, Charles, since you left,' she said, when I had settled down on the dry leaves by her side.

I replied that I hoped Aunt Georgina had given me a good character.

'Not altogether. She said you had lost your youth before you had time to enjoy it.'

'No! I did enjoy it. Vienna, America, a profession which I loved – Good Lord, I knew I was having the time of my life!'

'I suppose she meant that you couldn't pick it up again.'

I agreed that she probably did and was prepared to leave it at that.

'Don't you ever feel that you belong here now?'

Her great, heavily-lashed grey eyes were on me and forced me into sincerity. I pointed to the sweep of the turf, the golden stone walls and a church tower rising above the trees in a distant valley, all delicate and unreal in the beginning of the clear evening light. I told her how often in my ride I had thought of this as *her* country, each pervading the other, and how I longed to come out of my spiritual forests and could not. I tried to explain that I thought of myself as a European living gladly and appreciatively in England but that I had no real right to the union of love.

'Why on earth not?' she asked. 'You have earned every right.'

'I haven't earned anything.'

'Georgina has told me all about you, Charles,' she replied impatiently. 'The Austrian underground and the Gestapo and the rescue of the women from Ravensbruck. And then you wouldn't even take our George Cross. You are the most absurdly proud man I ever came across!'

I must admit I had never thought of myself as proud, and I said so.

She let me have it. No sweet seventeen about her at all. She reminded me of a falcon suddenly loosed from the fist: a lovely, brooding thing detonated into a bronze and silver arrow of energy.

'You're still a boy,' she accused me. 'You've never got over being the Graf von Dennim. You won't admit there is anything higher than that. What you do is what you think a Dennim ought to do. You never take. You never give other people a chance. It's all giving, giving, giving by your own laws and nobody else's. I wish to God the Dennims still owned half Europe or whatever they did own. And then perhaps you could just be content with giving away material things and not be too proud to have to hide yourself in squirrels and that damned horse.'

'About Nur Jehan,' I said, firmly changing the subject after a silence. 'We all accept so much nonsense without thinking. Of course he can be ridden by a woman!'

'Who has ridden him?'

'No one yet. But the cause is simple. Your legs aren't long enough.'

'No?' she asked, looking along the slim length of her outstretched jodhpurs until she arrived at her toes.

'For Nur Jehan, I mean,' I replied desperately. 'And Georgina's legs are shorter still. He has a very sensitive rib – from an old wound probably. My heel goes behind and below it. Yours doesn't and a boy's wouldn't. But your father and I have long legs, and so, I expect, did his former owner.'

I think Benita then remarked that it was delightful how kind old maids and bachelors were to animals, but I do not remember.

I am compelled to dehumanize her. I find that in writing autobiography you cannot please a woman. You are bound to say too much or too little for her. Benita complains with reason that I have devoted far more space to Nur Jehan than to her. But when I have ventured upon more detailed description either of her or of that late afternoon in the windbreak outside the barn, down comes the censorship upon my pages. She insists and very rightly that it is nobody's business but our own.

And there was I with my utterly misplaced chivalry! I made one last effort by calmly identifying myself with the old maids and bachelors. We knew very well, I said, that we had plenty to give to an animal, but were too humble to believe we had much left to offer our fellows.

'Too proud,' she answered. 'Suppose you or I died tonight which would be older than the other?'

That was the end of my self-control. It should, of course, have doubled it. After all, I was quite likely to die that night – which was by far the best of all my reasons for pretending to Benita that my affection for her was fatherly. But I was so moved that I behaved like a boy of twenty who believes that no one has ever known such love before. And why the devil not? I very often do believe it.

It was after seven when Nur Jehan and her pony cantered

along the top of the plateau and down to the east. At the main road Benita insisted that Nur Jehan's day had been long enough and that he should not walk the six miles to Stow-on-the-Wold and back again.

I accepted the excuse, though I knew the stallion was not in the least tired. It was best that we should separate quickly. On the way down through cut woodland, where hazel and elder grew close to the path, I had once heard another horse. There was nothing surprising in that, but I had to know who was the rider – and I was not going to revive her memories of the valley below the Wen Acre Plantation by suddenly playing Red Indians through the undergrowth and leaving her with the impression that her future husband was in need of a psychiatrist.

To avoid the close cover I took Nur Jehan straight up the bare, sharp slope and back towards the barn along high ground. The long fields were still bathed in light and deserted as a prairie. The routine of the farms was over for the day.

I too felt permeated by the light. Benita brought this dear land with her just as surely as if she had been heiress to a thousand acres. I could neither analyse nor recognize myself. It is a startling rebirth to begin living in the future after ten years of obsession with the past. I found myself thinking of the economics of marriage with all the responsibility of a sound young man at the beginning of his career. I was at the beginning in a way. I had never bothered with half a dozen different appointments which were quite certainly within my reach. The next one with a decent salary would be mine. That and her pencil – any zoologist would jump at the chance of getting her as an illustrator – would keep us in reasonable comfort for a start. I smiled with amusement at my own dreaming.

'Good evening, sir! That is a splendid animal.'

Hearty, perfectly in keeping with his surroundings, the man rode out of a little covert of thorn on the edge of the escarpment. He appeared to have just passed through it. There was nothing to suggest that he had watched me take leave of Benita, noted my route back and waited for me.

His face was strong and casual. If I had not seen him before

I might never have noticed its quality of intentness. He wore a bowler hat, breeches and boots, a faultless jacket. The bushy eyebrows were not there. My guess that they had been stuck on was right; their purpose was to prevail as the dominant point in any description of him. Nor was his hair dark any more. It was white, prematurely white. Yet we had all called him the dark gentleman. He looked older and more distinguished than at Hernsholt. He was riding a chestnut mare, a Cotswold hunter of sixteen hands, up to his weight and with powerful quarters.

My start disconcerted Nur Jehan. In collecting the stallion I managed to collect myself.

'Good evening, sir!' I replied.

How right I had been to tackle him in my own way! He was indeed above suspicion. Even if I could have proved that he had taken a room in my street, the police would be almost bound to accept his innocent explanation of it. It was inconceivable that he should have blown a postman in half, murdered Sporn and Weber and ingeniously kept Dickfuss praying three days for death before he allowed him to die. I could have sworn the man was a magistrate and in the running for Sheriff of the county.

'Are you going far?' he asked.

'Just exercising.'

It would have been the end of me if I had admitted that I was bound directly for the lonely clump of trees on the horizon half a mile ahead where, as he must have known, I was camping. My only hope was to keep him off and lead him, without arousing any suspicion, suddenly down to the world of farms and villages. He had caught me on the only evening when I had for a moment forgotten him. I was completely at his mercy. I had no chance of beating him to the draw, since the clumsy holster of the Mauser was under my left arm-pit.

'A worthwhile job,' he said cordially. 'Of course we have all heard of you and Nur Jehan.'

'You live here?' I asked.

'No. I am just staying with friends.'

His manners were pleasant and assured. Evidently he had not the least idea that I had recognized him. Inside me I was screaming to myself that if he killed me he was doomed, that my friends knew enough about him to establish his identity, and that I must tell him so. But would he think it true? Was it in fact true? There was no evidence against him but mine. And I was not going to be alive to give it.

He came up on my right, for he had to. We were now walking our horses side by side. Imperceptibly the pace slowed. I could not allow him to drop behind and shoot me through the back, but I could not stop without some explanation. I could not even sit up, touch Nur Jehan with my heel and bolt for it. True, I might get clear. I was familiar enough with his character to know that he never took a chancy shot. But the fellow was an experienced horseman; he would spot at once that it was deliberate flight. It was quite possible that he would raise his bowler hat ironically and vanish – to reappear on some other evening when love had made me careless at whatever home I shared with Benita.

'He is only half trained,' I said in order to put the blame for any sudden move on Nur Jehan. 'He was brought up as a pet.'

'Yes. Always disastrous. Is he excitable?'

'No. And your mare?'

He was evasive. He did not know. That proved at any rate that the mare did not belong to him. He was the sort of man who would unhesitatingly be lent a good horse.

Whatever move I made must not be obvious. It must appear to this purring tiger that Nur Jehan was solely responsible. I sat loosely and continued to chat. Then I drove my left heel hard into the stallion's tender rib and prayed that I wouldn't be thrown.

Nur Jehan failed me. Instead of bucking or bolting, he snorted, shook his head and continued to walk. He clearly liked the horse alongside him and was not going to be deterred from a promising acquaintanceship by carelessness on the part of his rider.

My companion noticed nothing, for he could not see my left leg and I had not gathered my horse. I tried it again. This time Nur Jehan stopped dead, offended and puzzled. He did not particularly resent pressure which he felt to be accidental; what he would not stand was deliberate use of a sore rib to give orders. But the friend on his back was sitting easily and not giving any orders. The circumstances were all wrong.

This considerate rider also stopped. That was what I dreaded and had been trying to avoid. Unless we were to stay there all night I had to start first and allow him to remain for a decisive second or two behind me. I played the inefficient horseman and sawed at Nur Jehan's mouth, who began to dance.

'Completely untrainable!' I shouted angrily.

'Weren't you perhaps a little hard on his mouth?'

'Damn his mouth!'

'Patience, my dear sir!' advised my executioner very pleasantly. 'Patience always leads to the result you want in the end.'

He had now started to ride with half his right hand stuffed carelessly into his outside coat pocket. He went ahead for a moment and crossed my path on the excuse of looking closely at some sheep which he pretended to admire. He made it extremely difficult for me to avoid coming up on his right. Riding side by side in that position I had no defence against a shot through the pocket and into the liver – or into anywhere if the unseen weapon were of sufficient calibre to knock me off my horse.

To follow him and come up on his left was awkward, but Nur Jehan's behaviour was perfect. He danced just enough to disguise the fact that the edging to the left was deliberate. We rode on over the turf, both breaking from canter to walk a little abruptly but not so unreasonably as to be unnatural. I had an irrelevant and vivid vision of some gymkhana or riding school – so long ago that I could not remember which and certainly did not try – at which I had to turn an obstinate pony among posts. This despairing exercise upon which I was now engaged had equally simple rules. Come up on your companion's right, and you are dead. But you must not be caught avoiding it, nor he trying to force you into it.

The icy sweat which had been dripping down my ribs and over my too imaginative liver was under control. I was a trifle more confident. This man, as I suspected, was not a gambler; otherwise he would have brought his hand up and across the saddle. He had the experience to know it was not so easy as for the cow-hands of fiction. At the appearance of the pistol, the target would start, the horse between the target's legs following the movement of alarm enough to throw off the aim. I myself could have taken the risk. I would have waited for horse and man to steady and still been sure of killing even if the range had opened to ten yards.

That one advantage – though largely imaginary – cheered me a little. And now came another. The man was losing that patience of which he had boasted.

'A wonderful spot for a gallop,' he invited.

It was. Nur Jehan was most unlikely to hold off the challenge of that powerful mare. From my companion's point of view nothing could stop him overhauling his victim close enough to touch the unsuspecting back with the barrel. But I was not unsuspecting, and he had given me a slim chance. I had to take it, and hope for an opportunity to change direction – down to the farms and human eyes.

I had allowed Nur Jehan a few healthy gallops, but never before had I ridden him flat out. My little Persian Arab was off like a greyhound from a trap, a start with which the heavier mare could not compete at all. My low voice and knees must have communicated to him an urgency which demanded response.

After a hundred yards I looked round. The mare was coming up on my left and ten to twenty paces behind. Nur Jehan seemed to be holding his own, though how much of it he had gained at the start I could not tell. Three hundred yards. Nearly four hundred yards. And then a stone wall, new and without a gap, which meant that I must pull him up.

But away to the right were the chimneys of a cotttage and safety. Could Nur Jehan jump? What could he jump? At least he had managed to get over the untidy hedges of Gillon's Glebe meadow. But if he hit a Cotswold wall it was the end of the pair of us. A pistol shot wouldn't be necessary. A stone while I was lying on the ground would do the job neatly and leave no evidence of murder.

I did not dare to steady the stallion. I made my intention

plain and sat still. Nur Jehan, wildly excited, took off a couple of yards too soon. There was only the faintest click as a hind shoe touched the wall, and he was away again in his stride.

I swung off to the right into a wide grass track leading down hill between wire fences. Once there I could dictate the closeness and position of my companion. I looked over my shoulder in time to see him check the mare and jump compactly. Then he broke into an easy canter as if waiting for me to come back and join him.

I pulled up Nur Jehan and also waited. I was safe. A farmer and some white-coated vet or inspector were examining bullocks in the next field. The upper windows of the cottage which had showed only a tall chimney were in full view. I leaned forward to pat Nur Jehan's neck, and under cover of the movement extracted the Mauser from its awkward holster and tucked it inside my shirt with the barrel down the waistband of my breeches. It was very uncomfortable and hindered riding at any pace but a walk. I felt confident, however, that from then on if the tiger drew any kind of lethal weapon he would still have his paw in plaster when he came up for trial.

As I showed no sign of moving from where I was, he joined me.

'A remarkable burst of speed for an untrained Arab,' he said genially. 'I thought you were down at that wall. But, my dear sir, what a risk to take!'

'He was bolting,' I replied. 'He might have charged right into it.'

That earned me a slow, penetrating look, but I had the answer ready to avert suspicion.

'I have no curb, you see,' I explained. 'He is not accustomed to it. But of course we should not have allowed you to tempt us.'

I asked him to come down and have a drink with me. Now that I was momentarily safe, contact had to be maintained. I might be able to manoeuvre him into making an attack before witnesses, or I might discover his identity and regain the initiative.

We walked our horses down to the village below. The only

evidence of its existence was a carpet of great tree-tops, the roof of a Jacobean manor and the church tower which I had pointed out to Benita in, as it now seemed, some former life. My companion chatted easily and amicably. He was a superb actor. I should have been left unaccountably dead upon the empty turf above us if I had not been able to take that long look through the hedge on the road from Stoke to Hernsholt and watch his face when it had been undisguisedly intent upon revenge.

The village street was fairly deserted. It was broad enough to hold a small country market and gently curving, with perhaps thirty houses on one side, divided by the inn, and twenty on the other, divided by the church. All were of stone and none – except for a village school in false Gothic – was later than the eighteenth century. The low sun brought out the gold of the Cotswold masonry and tiles.

'They are the most beautiful villages in Europe,' said my companion.

I answered at once that they were, and was surprised that my reply had not been in the least conventional. The Tyrol? Spain? Alsace? Would I have agreed unhesitatingly the day before, or was this the influence of Benita? I confirmed that the essential button of my shirt was undone and the butt of the Mauser free. It would be disgraceful to die just when my eyes had become English.

A short lane led us along the side of the inn to its yard. There was a garage but no stable. We hitched our horses to the railings and went into the yard, where the flagstones had been roughly diversified by a few rock plants and stone troughs. There were two iron chairs and a rustic table for any customers who preferred to drink in the open.

My companion walked straight to the table and sat down. I remained standing and asked him what he would take.

'It doesn't matter,' he answered, and then, as if aware of the oddness of his reply, added with more animation: 'Whisky. Scotch, if you will be so good.'

I had to turn my back on him in order to enter the garden door of the pub. I didn't like it, but hoped the windows which overlooked us would keep him out of temptation. When I returned from the bar with a tray, both hands occupied, I carefully observed the position of the other pair of hands. They were both on the table and looked a little unnatural. Left alone to do some thinking, he may have come to the conclusion that I did not accept strangers so trustfully as it appeared. That jumping of the wall, that bearing to the right and safety could well have been deliberate.

With drinks on the table, I pretended to drop my matches and stooped to pick them up. The Mauser was now on my lap. I was sitting opposite to him and it could not be seen. My coat hid it from the bar window. I drank half my whisky and noticed that my fellow horseman merely touched the glass to his lips.

'Your name is von Dennim, isn't it?' he asked.

'Dennim. I have dropped the *von*.'

'Yes, I can understand it. When you have finished your drink may I ride back with you to the top of the hill?'

I asked him if that was his way home. He replied, still quite pleasantly, that it was not, but that he wished for more of my company. He stressed the word 'wish'. If I were thinking of escape, I should recognize it as an order. If I were still unsuspicious, there was nothing to frighten me in the slight arrogance of tone.

This was the end. The tiger had committed himself. I could act.

'Lower your head to pick up, for example, your handkerchief,' I told him, 'and you will observe that I too have you covered. My legs are crossed and I am sitting sideways. From under the table you can only give me a painful wound. If I see the slightest sign of you raising that pistol above it, I will kill you. Is that clear?'

He looked at me with such a blaze of hatred that I was on the very edge of firing. Very gradually madness died away and was replaced by an ironical detachment far more in keeping with the face.

'So you know what I have to say to you?'

'What you said to Sporn, Dickfuss and Weber. But the game is up.'

'The game is not up, von Dennim. As you say – or did you say it? – you dare not shoot first.'

I pointed out that he had an automatic in his hand, that I should be justified in killing him and acquitted.

'Perhaps,' he answered coolly. 'Only perhaps. It is going to be very hard to connect me with any of those executions. However frightened you are, I do not think you will shoot first.'

I was astonished to find that I was no longer particularly frightened.

'If this is stalemate, as you think,' I said, 'you may as well tell me what you have against me. You were never in Buchenwald.'

'No – but my wife was.'

'There were no women.'

'Except by invitation.'

I could not understand. My expression must have been exasperatingly patronizing.

'Have you forgotten, von Dennim? Did it mean so little to you? Very well, I will remind you. I like each one of you to know why you are going to die. The Buchenwald officers used certain women from the camp at Ravensbruck for their amusement, did they not? You yourself once fetched a little party of them.'

It was perfectly true. I had conceived the scheme and timed it carefully and at last got the opportunity of fetching such a party from the women's concentration camp. But I still did not see what it had to do with him or his wife. This was the incident which had brought Olga Coronel over to London after the war to thank me, when she and Georgina decided – rightly, I expect – that I was not in a state to see anyone who could remind me too vividly of the past.

It had been the custom of that unspeakable swine, Major Sporn, to borrow occasionally these unfortunate creatures from Ravensbruck. Besides the political prisoners awaiting the Ravensbruck gas chamber, there were plenty of common criminals utterly demoralized and only too glad of a break in their half-starved lives and a chance to drink themselves into a stupor.

On the afternoon when I myself went to Ravensbruck I slipped into my busload of gipsies, thieves and prostitutes, Catherine Dessayes and Olga Coronel. They knew that they were to trust me, and that was all. Twelve women had left for Buchenwald, filthy, dishevelled, gaudily painted. But was it ten or twelve who arrived?

Sporn, already drunk, didn't know and didn't care. I, pretending also to be drunk, had juggled with the two extra – subtracted them, added them, done everything but multiply them. Forty-eight hours later Dessayes and Coronel had been picked up at a secret landing-ground and were in hospital in London. Meanwhile I was under arrest; but they couldn't see how I had worked the trick and they shot the wrong man. At least he was the wrong man from their point of view. Otherwise they could not have chosen a more deserving candidate.

'Your wife could not have been among those women,' I said.

'She was, von Dennim. I know something of what they did to her in every week from her arrest to her death. The men who interrogated her were hanged as war criminals – all but one whom I hanged myself. With Major Sporn and Captain Dickfuss I had the pleasure of dealing when they had served their sentences. And in the course of my conversation with Dickfuss I learned that I had a debt to pay to Weber and you. It took me some time to find you. I should have guessed you were the type to save yourself by making friends with British Intelligence.'

'What did she look like?' I asked, ignoring this.

'She had long, dark hair,' he said. 'Her skin was very pale and transparent even in health.'

The corners of his heavy, mobile mouth twitched twice. He glared at me across the table with eyes in which the obsession of blood-feud had long taken the place of sorrow.

I remembered. The hair had been cut short, but the transparency of the skin was unforgettable. They had housed her, I suppose, among the dregs of the camp in order that she should disappear from all human knowledge. God alone knew how they had drugged and broken her before she was ever interned in Ravensbruck. When I saw her she did not seem to know where she was or to care. She was already dead, though physically in apparent good health.

'What had she done?'

'Done! What had she done? You scum, does the name of Savarin mean anything to you?'

I asked him peaceably if he were Savarin.

'I was.'

Presumably some of the French knew to whom that cover name belonged. London never did, nor, I believe, did the enemy. A leader of the Resistance, incredibly astute and merciless, Savarin had carried on his own private war against the German occupiers. His every act of bloodshed and sabotage carried the stamp of his own temperament – a sardonic savagery which belonged to some sultan of the Arabian Nights.

'But those women,' I began, 'were . . .'

I stopped. I was only making matters worse. And I found unbearable the thought of the revenge which the Gestapo had taken when they suspected that they had caught the wife of Savarin. Dessayes and Coronel could never have known of her presence in Ravensbruck since she was not interned among the politicals. If those two gallant women had guessed that she was in the bus, one of them would have insisted on her escape and given up her own life instead.

'Dickfuss and Sporn I can understand,' I said. 'But why did you kill Hans Weber?'

'He went with you and drove the bus.'

Accurate again. Weber was the officer in charge of transport. I had persuaded him to drive for the sake of his quite remarkable stupidity. If a total of ten were repeated to him often enough he could be trusted to swear to it.

'You might as well have executed the man who made it!' I exclaimed.

I was overwhelmed by the cruelty and pity of the thing. I knew I could never kill Savarin in cold blood. To take revenge for acts of revenge was merely to extend the horror and call it justice.

I suppose no man who has given great love to a woman

worthy of love could ever guarantee that he would not kill the devils who destroyed her. But on the spur of the moment. To wait ten years without losing, in spite of the wear and tear of sane daily life, the compulsion to avenge her must be rare. And yet not so rare a few centuries ago. I am no psychologist, but I think the true parallel is religious mania. In Savarin's case the wrathful god was his own very real but perverted sense of honour. He felt that he *ought* to kill, that he was morally bound to kill and that he must never permit himself to fall into any backsliding. To that, of course, must be added a pleasure in killing. He must always have had a powerful streak of sadistic cruelty – perhaps sublimated in youth but during the war magnificently released and justified by patriotism.

I was tempted to turn my back on him and ride away. That was how my father would have dismissed him, ignoring his existence at the possible expense of his own. A contemptuous and honourable way out of the dilemma. Pride, Benita would call it. The day before I, too, might have turned my back. But the future was no longer my own to relinquish.

I told him that it was the end, and that he must surrender. I disclosed to him all I knew – how he had tried to poison me in my cottage, how he had watched me from the old air-raid shelter and left his horse with Fred Gorble, how I had so nearly trapped him before a witness at the badger sett.

His face hardly changed. I had the impression that he had considered all that over and over again, but rejected it as unlikely.

'Watching badgers down wind,' he said to himself more than to me. 'I should have known that even the Gestapo could not be so stupid.'

So that was why he had instinctively suspected something wrong and avoided the obvious line of approach!

'You might have known, too,' I retorted, 'that an authority on squirrels can spot the difference between the French and English varieties.'

That, I could see, at last disturbed him. The purchase of the squirrels which he had let loose in the Wen Acre Plantation was just the sort of evidence which police could trace.

'Do you understand now, Savarin,' I asked, 'that if you force me to shoot I can plead self-defence?'

He understood all right, but he was beyond caring. This was the tiger I predicted, who would still come on even if a bullet had raked his body.

'I should be sorry not to be present at your trial,' he answered with a calm which was no less deadly for being artificial. 'I am half English and was educated here. I know the English criminal law. No one will believe you, von Dennim, and my friends are influential enough to see that you are tried for murder. There will be several weeks – separated by a period in gaol – while your past comes out. It will interest the charming girl to whom you were very properly saying good-bye. I should think you will have to change your name. A von Dennim in the Gestapo! The head of your distinguished family should kill you if I do not.'

'I *am* the Graf von Dennim,' I answered.

He jerked forward his body and spat in my face.

From that point on it was another person who took command. I neither approve nor disapprove of him. What he did is what I should do again in similar circumstances. But my normally quiet self recognizes him with difficulty.

I shook with self-control and heard myself saying:

'I have a right to know with whom I must deal. Your identity matters no longer.'

'The Vicomte de Saint Sabas.'

I knew the name – and on one point more intimately than the historians who watch down the centuries the inevitable and unruly appearance of a Saint Sabas whenever the nobles of France are trumpeting defiance to the King of England or their own.

'You have a son?' I asked.

'I have.'

'My conscience is easier.'

'You are impertinent!'

'No, sir. The first Saint Sabas was a steward of the Dennims and ennobled by us. So I did not wish to end the family. I cannot help the disgrace.'

'Disgrace?'

The word stung him a lot more than my medieval absurdity – which, anyway, he knew to be true. I explained it.

'You murdered an innocent postman, Saint Sabas. Was that an execution too? Chicago style?'

'An accident!' he exploded. 'How the devil could I foresee it?'

His right arm began to move. Slightly quicker the barrel of the Mauser was over the edge of the table. Both weapons returned to the lap.

I told him the true story of my war. It was fair that the man should be given a chance to believe. But the facts seemed to make no impression at all on those impatient and contemptuous eyes. How could they? If he had accepted them, he would have had to face his own guilt.

'My reply to that is that you are a liar and a coward,' he said. 'Not even Dickfuss thought of claiming to be a British agent.'

I finished my drink and disregarded the minor insult. I remarked – though, as I say, it wasn't a self I knew which was speaking – that it was difficult to arrange conditions between a liar and a madman, but that I would make a suggestion.

I was well aware of the suicidal folly of what this damned Graf von Dennim was about to propose. But I could see no other way out. I refused to kill Saint Sabas in cold blood. And if I made the slightest move from that table towards the back door of the pub or towards Nur Jehan, Saint Sabas would kill me. At least our ancestors could get us out of the stalemate when nothing else could.

'I give you no conditions,' he said.

'Then you may accept mine. You know the barn in its clump of trees. We will ride towards it together but out of pistol shot. We will halt three hundred yards from it.

'I shall stay where I am, giving you time to examine the barn thoroughly since I know it and you do not. You will then retire to a distance of three hundred yards on the other side. We shall still be in sight of each other and can know if the terms are observed.'

'How do I know you will not ride off and hide in a police station?'

'How do I know you won't vanish? Savarin has a lot of practice in changing his name and appearance.'

'You know it because I intend to kill you. I am impatient, von Dennim.'

His voice rose a little above its usual cold tone. He was savagely impatient.

That was my motive, too, I said. I did not intend to spend the rest of my life examining my food and parcels.

He still refused to accept. He had no fear of dying, only of dying before he could kill. I knew that, but I accused him of being afraid. He was quite unmoved.

'Yes,' he said. 'I am afraid you will run.'

This was getting beyond endurance. I felt an appalling, nervous desire to laugh. The Graf von Dennim and the zoologist were each finding the other ridiculous, with the result that both were near hysteria.

'You spat in my face,' I said. 'Shall I put it this way for you? That even if a von Dennim is a Gestapo officer and a Saint Sabas murders postmen, each has a tradition in spite of it.'

He looked at me with less assurance, or at any rate with less intensity of hatred. He was human again – the deliberate, discriminating judge of what his victim was likely to do.

'You are different from the rest,' he said, 'I will agree to your conditions.'

I stood up with my back to the windows of the inn and slipped the Mauser into its holster. Saint Sabas wavered, and I had a clear view of his weapon. It was a .45 automatic. The Dennim family held his eyes contemptuously for me, while the familiar self disapproved in abject panic of this highly dangerous theatre. He put on the safety catch and dropped the pistol into his outside pocket.

We walked side by side to our horses without a word. The atmosphere of formality seemed to be working. The few horsy villagers who watched us must, I am sure, have assumed that the two beautifully mounted middle-aged men were old friends who chose to be silent.

When we were alone and back on the green road which led to the hill top, we separated. Each kept close to the fence on his own side with twenty yards of turf and ruts between the horses. Nur Jehan strongly objected.

'There is no reason to fight your horse,' Saint Sabas said. 'What little beauty is in this world has already suffered enough from you. I will give you my word of honour that you may safely ride by my side, and I will accept yours.'

I thanked him, and added:

'The light is going fast.'

'It was too clear this evening. It looks like rain.'

'Not before midnight, I should say.'

'It has certainly been a remarkable June.'

'Yes. We have both been fortunate in our weather.'

'It would interest me to know one thing. All along you invited this meeting, von Dennim?'

'I did.'

'No police at all in it?'

There was a limit to confidence. I was not going to tell him that.

'What they are doing you probably know as well as I do, Saint Sabas.'

'My French blood tells,' he said with a harsh laugh. 'At one moment I am overwhelmed by the cunning of the British. At the next I am certain that all the cunning is invented by myself.'

The hill top was now bare and dismal under the overcast sky. There was just enough wind to sing faintly in the telephone wires which marched up the hill along with us and ended at the last house. The barn and the wide clump of trees were no longer sinister as they had been in sunlight. Set in the greater loneliness of the uplands, they suggested shelter and a roof.

'I doubt if we shall be able to see each other at six hundred yards,' I said.

'I will signal to you with a torch when I am in position.'

'Mine, I am afraid, is in my rucksack at the barn.'

'It works?' he asked.

'Yes, very well.'

'Take this, then! I will pick up yours when I examine the barn.'

Saint Sabas handed over his torch, and with a slight inclination of the head rode forward to the clump of trees.

I returned his bow. It is possible that the exchange of torches was as near as he could bring himself to a salute. Religious maniacs – if I am right in my fanciful explanation of him – can be very pleasant people so long as the subject of damnation does not come up. But at the time I was divided between admiration of his manners and suspicion that he intended to tamper with my rucksack. I dismissed it. Whatever century we were in, both of us were in it. And in any case the time for assassination by drugs or explosives had passed.

Dusk and the trees swallowed up Saint Sabas. I dismounted and thought over what my tactics were going to be. There could be no more doubts whether I had a moral right to kill him. I had not a dog's chance of living if I didn't, and it was pointless even to worry about my legal position. I was empty of anger and mercy alike. If it had just been a question of losing my own life, I might still have had some trouble with conscience; but it was my future with Benita which was at stake, and that was a very different matter from my future with squirrels. The first shot must deliver us from any more fear, and no damned nonsense about it.

Fieldcraft and silent feet were all I had to put against his speed and desperation. Savarin must have had as much battle experience as any long-lived infantry platoon sergeant, while I myself, though I had been under fire, had no experience of attack. His other overwhelming advantage was that he did not care whether he died or not so long as I did. The game was up for him. Too many people had seen him with me. The most he could ever hope for was the life of a fugitive if he were able to get out of England before my body was found.

The obvious first move was to get into the thick belt of trees around the barn and let the other fellow do the attacking: in fact, to hold the interior lines. Saint Sabas would not see any objection, for he knew nothing whatever of my history. Right up to that evening he had assumed that I was just a discreditable member of the Dennim family; there were plenty to choose from, especially among the Bavarian branch, and some of them had been Nazis. So he had no reason to suspect that under the trees I was likely to be his master.

Very well. I could reckon on his riding hard and straight for the windbreak and then lying up in cover, rather than taking advantage of his well-trained mare and attacking me in the open.

Far away across the empty plateau I saw the torch winking at me. I mounted Nur Jehan and answered. Saint Sabas charged into sight along the line I expected, and I, instead of racing him for the trees and getting the whole width of the cover between us, galloped off on a tangent to the right of the windbreak. The range closed to a hundred yards as he held his course, but the light was more deceptive than I anticipated. I dropped to the ground, fired and grazed – for the shadowy figure raised a hand to his neck or ear – fired again and missed. Horse and man vanished into the trees.

That was that. At the cost of some slight loss of blood he had won the interior lines, and my plan of dropping him clean in the open had landed me in the worst possible position. It was unlikely that I would ever have another chance to use my longer range and greater accuracy unless Saint Sabas were caught on the move by the sudden appearance of the moon. It was up, showing faintly through the drifting clouds and occasionally unobscured.

I was out of the effective range of his .45 automatic. It was a better weapon than mine, however, for hand-to-hand fighting in semi-darkness, and I now had to close with it. The only safe move was to crawl away quickly until I was part of the hillside and then enter the windbreak wherever shadows and ground permitted approach. He could not guard all his perimeter.

But couldn't he? I reckoned that I could guard the perimeter very easily when I myself chose for my night's lodging the isolated copse. I did not fancy stalking that inscrutable wall of twilight from any direction whatever. The ground sloped gently away from the trees and was bare turf.

Though I had been telling myself again and again that I must not let him break contact, I should have been very glad at the moment if some belated shepherd or gamekeeper had come up the hill and frightened him off. But there was little chance of that. The nearest cottages were half a mile away and sheltered from direct sound by the contours of the hill. Even if the two cracks of the Mauser were carried sharply on the wind they need not necessarily attract attention. Somewhere to the east on lower ground, perhaps belonging to the lady with the dogs, three or four guns had been out after wood-pigeon coming in to roost. There were also cherry orchards, well down on the Worcester-shire side, banging away all night with their bird alarms. Those exasperating charges had once made me dive for cover near Chipping Marton, when fortunately Benita was not with me. Farmers set them to go off at intervals during the twenty-four hours and had – or said they had – no means of putting them out of action after dark.

I heard Saint Sabas cantering on through the windbreak. He was now presumably tying his mare to a tree. I had nothing to which I could tether Nur Jehan. He stayed close, but was thoroughly uneasy and restless. He was not grazing. At any rate – and that was a blessing – he was not in the affectionate mood to follow his rider about.

There was probably time to run boldly for the trees, but I had learned to take no gambles in a hurry against Savarin. I re-mained cuddling the butt of the Mauser and thinking out the end game of this blind chess which we had played for the last three weeks. As soon as he was at the edge of the windbreak – and he might well have turned his mare loose and be there already – he should be able to see Nur Jehan close to the point where I had flung myself off and fired. He would not expect me, too, still to be close. But I would be. The ground helped.

A slight fold led obliquely to the clump of trees. It was hardly visible as a depression at all, but on the rim were nine-inch stems of seeding grass, just tall enough in that light to be a screen rather than a guide to my movements. I rolled over into it.

Hoping that he was now straining his eyes in the wrong direc-tion, I slowly followed the fold closer and closer to the trees. When I had reached a point fifteen yards out, there was nothing for it but to rush the rest across the open. But I was not much afraid of that. Thick cloud was blowing.

I started to leave my cover. I had already drawn a leg under me ready for the spring and raised my head when I was fairly caught by the erratic moon. I lay still, praying that Saint Sabas was not on my side of the trees at all and well aware that, if he was, the dark blotch of my body could be made out. His shot – a carefully aimed shot to judge by the infernal delay – plunged into the turf alongside my ribs. I cried out, kicked myself straight and rolled back into the fold of the ground I had just left.

His years as Savarin had probably taught him the difference of sound between a bullet in turf and a bullet in flesh. But at that range I doubted if he could have heard the strike at all; the report would cover it. There was a good chance, if my cry had been convincing enough, that he would come up cautiously to administer the *coup de grâce*.

Silence went on and on for what seemed all of half an hour. I did not dare stir. At last I heard him on the move. He was some-where in the middle of the trees near the barn. That indicated a doubt in his mind. He was not going to leave cover opposite my body; he was going to approach from some unexpected angle. I still felt, however, that he could approach from any angle he liked. If he meant to fire a last shot into the copse I had him.

Saint Sabas mounted his mare. I heard the creak of leather and the jingle of the bit. Was he so convinced of the effect of his shot that he intended to ride off? But that was out of character. So I decided that he was bluffing. If he could persuade me he had gone, I should get pretty tired of lying still to no purpose and soon show whether I was alive or not.

Distances were short and it was all very quick. He seemed to be cantering round the windbreak towards me. I assumed that he meant to come into sight just out of easy range and ride away. He came closer still, now just inside the trees, offering a possible shot; but I had had enough of moving targets in the dusk and it was not worth while to raise my head and look at him. There would be time enough for action when the sound of the hooves stopped or passed on.

They did neither. Man and horse burst out of the copse and

charged me, Saint Sabas leaning low over the mane. I had not a hope. I was clinging to my tiny fold of ground as if I had been flattened into it by a roller. There was no chance to fire. By the time I had changed position and begun to elevate the barrel they were on me.

Shot on the ground or trampled into it. I chose the latter. But the good mare of course put her feet where I was not. And that was all the more to her credit since Saint Sabas must have been already reining her in. When I was half up he had already wheeled her round and was on me again.

I jinked like a snipe. My only cover was the mare herself. I cannot explain in any detail what happened. At one moment I was under her chest and hanging on to the martingale with one hand while trying to thrust the Mauser into a pocket with the other. I had released the awkward holster-butt. I don't know how or when.

Looking back at it in cold blood, I think I should have shot the mare. That I didn't was not due to any compunction. I repeat – she was the only cover I had. She was precious. As I saw it then, he could kill me as she fell to her knees or while he was coming off.

If he had had a sabre he could have cut me down three times over. A .45 Colt from a frantic, rearing horse was a less reliable weapon. Where the shots went I do not know, but they didn't hit. One nicked the point of the shoulder, for I remember vividly the smell of burnt hair and I think I saw a streak of blood. That was the end. The mare shied and fought him, and I was into the trees before he could regain control.

I dropped on to the carpet of beech leaves gasping for breath. To be at the receiving end of a cavalry charge is not a sport for a man in his forties. It took me some time to realize that I was unhurt, and longer still before my hand was steady enough to shoot. I told myself that honours were even. Saint Sabas had found out with little risk to himself that I was not dead. On the other hand I was safely in cover and could at last fight my battle under conditions which I understood. An optimistic view, but good for morale. If ever a man had been defeated, I had.

Now for the first time I realized that there was going to be no quick end to this duel. When I put forward my desperate proposal which allowed us at last to rise from that garden table I had imagined an affair of dishonour in the last of the daylight which ten minutes would settle. I did not foresee the low, grey cloud sweeping across the Cotswolds and bringing night half an hour too soon. My life was going to depend on chancy snap-shooting in darkness, and the question of ammunition supply was vital.

Had Saint Sabas got an extra magazine? Very improbable. He must have ridden out that afternoon assuming – if one could guess what murderers assumed – that one or, at the most, two shots would do. How many had he fired from his mare? Was it three or four? I was ashamed of not knowing, but it had seemed like a dozen. Only by counting the reports in my memory – as a man can count afterwards the number of times a single cylinder has fired though at the moment the roar was nearly continuous – could I work out the truth. It was four, plus his first shot from the edge of the trees. That left Saint Sabas three in his magazine against eight in the Mauser. Better say four in the magazine in case he started with one up the spout. And he would. By this time I knew him.

Both of us were now on foot and under the beeches. The windbreak was a rough oval with a diameter of a hundred and fifty yards one way and about a hundred the other. That sounds a small arena for terror and uncertainty, but visibility was down to twenty feet if the enemy moved and nothing at all if he didn't. Wherever a man lay down he automatically created an ambush. So, on the face of it, the odds were heavily against the attacker. But it was not much use to crouch and wait and switch a tail unless the prey could be attracted out of a thousand possible squares of darkness into the right one. And that meant that the defender had to make some noise while the attacker could afford to move silently.

The only moonlit space was the clearing in the centre of the copse which led to the barn. It gave an impression of being longer than it really was and looked like an avenue. At the head of it the entrance to the barn showed as a black arch, flanked on the left by a broken outline of black where were the remains of an old dung heap and a pile of rubble.

Saint Sabas was on the other side of this avenue. If he wanted to attack he had either to cross the open, which was suicide, or to work his way round the back of the barn into my side of the wood. I could faintly hear him on the move, so I decided to let him take the initiative.

I tip-toed silently to the back – the north side – of the barn where the belt of trees was narrow and waited for him to enter my territory. But he was up to that one. He left the trees and took to the open hillside, re-entering the wood behind me and in my half of it. He did not seem to be taking the precaution of moving silently, so I knew that he meant me to hear what he was doing. I could not make it out at all.

Had he decoyed me round to the back of the barn so that he could enter it by the door? I returned to the front and covered the door, though I had an uneasy instinct that the move was what he intended me to make and I paid more attention to my own security than to the threshold of the barn.

But he was nowhere near the barn. To my astonishment I saw him across the bottom of the clearing. He then started another round of the copse, sometimes out on the hillside, sometimes penetrating deeply into the trees. It was little use trying to intercept him or hunt him down. His movements were quite unpredictable.

This was nerve-racking. It only made sense on the theory that he was testing me to see if I were fool enough to fire at random. He used his mare, too – twice slapping her away to trot on her own through the darkness. I began to wonder if he had gone mad under the strain. This circling and darting back reminded me of an inefficient beater ordered to drive the game into the centre of the cover and thoroughly apprehensive about what might break back.

It was I, however, who was apprehensive and beginning to be fascinated. Tiger? He was more like a stoat or a weasel playing the fool in order to attract a bird's curiosity. Well, if he wanted me to come fluttering up to him, I was not going to.

His occasional dashes on the other side of the clearing took him nearer and nearer to the barn. So that was it, I thought; he meant to distract my attention so that he could get inside and make me winkle him out. The next time I heard him safely turning somersaults on the north side I crossed the front and dropped into the shadows of the old manure heap. As soon as another dash for the barn began, I crawled in and turned round to cover the edge of the trees and the doorway. I must admit I was thankful to be inside. I had never been asked to study forest fighting against the lunatic crashings of a poltergeist without a plan.

I suppose he continued beating the bounds for another quarter of an hour. Meanwhile, knowing that he was engaged outside, I took stock of the barn and freely used my torch in the corners which were out of sight of the doorway. During the afternoon I had merely glanced over the place with a view to making Nur Jehan comfortable, and had not examined it in detail.

In the left-hand wall as I faced the doorway was a long, narrow window, the sill of which was about six feet from the ground. A man entering from outside would make a good deal of noise, but it offered an easy way out from the inside, for there was a pile of loose hay beneath the window. The floor of the barn was fairly clear of obstructions, except for an old chaff-cutter, some bits of iron and baulks of timber which had been part of a cart, and a pile of hazel rods close to the door. Against the back wall were three dilapidated stalls for horses or cattle.

At last there was silence under the trees. I lay down a little back from the doorway preparing for the final shot. After a while I heard a horse walking placidly over the turf of the clearing towards me. I suspected that Saint Sabas was going to charge the door. It was not a bad idea if he thought that I was outside the barn and he wanted to get in through my covering fire. But I refused to be dazed by *haute-école* stuff this time and I was not going to be caught on the ground again.

I stood up to get a level shot, for I could not be seen in the pitch darkness. But there was no change of pace, no sudden rush. Nur Jehan, his lighter colour showing just in time through the grey-black of the entrance, walked into the barn, gave me a casual Judas kiss in passing and strolled into one of the stalls to see what, if anything, was in the manger. I prayed that Saint Sabas did not know his habits. If he did, Nur Jehan had given away the fact that I was in the barn.

A minute later the mare followed, sidling through the doorway and very nervous. She got mixed up with a pillar and an old cart shaft and let out at the lot with her heels. It was plain that Saint Sabas had driven her in to distract my attention – if I were inside – from his own approach. He succeeded in that. The crash made me as jumpy as the mare. I retreated a little from the door so that I could cover the window as well.

Then silence returned, broken only by the munching of the horses who had found something to their taste. Instinct told me that I ought to be really frightened, that the tiger was crouched for the spring. I refused to believe instinct. I could not afford to. Panic was very close. I kept on reminding myself that I must not risk being wounded and helpless. Saint Sabas had not the three days which he had spent on the punishment of Dickfuss, but no doubt he would gladly spare an hour.

At last I heard a scuffling on the stone sill of the window to my left. That was more cheerful. If he were climbing in, there had to be a moment when his head and shoulders would be silhouetted against the lighter night sky and it would be his last. My hand was perfectly steady in spite of the uncontrollable beating of the heart.

The scuffle stopped. When it began again it sounded like a slipping boot but was too high up. I moved a step or two back from the window to get a clearer field of fire and met an unexpected barrel hoop under the scattering of hay, which rustled as I gently extricated my foot. Out to my right a torch and a shot flashed, one as fast as the other – and too fast. I fired back to each side of the flash. There was no apparent effect. Six in the Mauser against three in the Colt.

I did not think I had scored. In the close quarters of the barn it was impossible to hear what the bullets had struck. Something long and light fell as I fired. It was one of the long hazel rods. Saint Sabas had used it for tickling the window sill. My instinct had been right. He was with me inside the barn.

So this was the position he wanted, where a savage recklessness would count for more than skill and a club be nearly as effective as a fire-arm. Now that it was too late his tactics made sense. The spectral referee of the two chess boards said nothing, but I was within a move of mate. All that aimless rushing about had been most effective psychological warfare, destroying my nerves until I was ready to seize upon any easy explanation of it.

He had indeed wanted to reach the barn, but not before he had hypnotized me into going inside it. He was not sure, I suppose, that I had really done so until Nur Jehan, fetched by him from the open hill, looked for and found me. Then the rest of his plan, the closing of the trap, came into operation. He had entered the barn crouched behind the mare's quarters. I should have remembered the cows and the stream.

My one idea now was to get out. That was partly due to shock at discovering myself so obedient to the enemy, partly to sheer terror because I dared not move so much as a coat sleeve in case he was within a couple of yards of me. I sank down slowly and squatted on my heels, afraid even so that a creak of the knees might give me away.

And then Nur Jehan screamed. It was utterly unnerving. A ghost or the sudden shriek of a mating vixen could not have been more weird and startling. I jumped round to face the horses without any regard at all for noise or cover. What in the devil's name was this loathsome ruse, and how had he done it? He would draw the line at getting under Nur Jehan's belly with a knife.

It was not till the stallion's second scream that I realized what was happening. The mare plunged out through the door, Nur Jehan after her. So that was the cause of his restlessness; and I had no doubt what had broken the inhibiting link between himself and the kindly creatures who played with him and tried to train him. It was the scent of human fear.

I dropped to the ground, streaming sweat. Mrs Melton's odd words came back to me: that the same fate was on the horse and the goat in the same place. I was near to tears with the poignancy of it. I wanted to live, as Nur Jehan would, to enjoy that fate.

'A fine foal, von Dennim, I should think. Ah well, in the midst of death we are in life.'

The panting, but still ironical voice came from the far end of the barn on the other side of the door. Under cover of the excitement he had slipped out of my half. The speed of my two shots must have shaken his confidence. It was comforting to know that he hated the threat of such incalculable close quarters as much as I did.

I was sure that this conversational opening meant that he wanted to know whether he had hit or not. It was a good moment to choose. One leaps at a human word when recovering from near hysteria. But I did not reply.

'They'll be very pleased at Chipping Marton, the vicar and all!' he went on. 'What a charming passionate child! Even a Gestapo officer will do at her age ... Missed again, von Dennim!'

The whine of a ricochet contemptuously emphasized it. I had been fool enough to fire two more shots at a voice certain to be under cover. Four in the Mauser now against three in the Colt.

A needed lesson. I reminded myself how I had made rings round this famous Savarin in the fields of Hernsholt. I must not be bluffed. I must never fire unless sure to hit. I must escape to the trees, and I must use my brains to get there. It was not going to be easy.

His night sight was as good as my own. If either of us attempted to crawl through the area of dark grey on the threshold of the door, he was dead. Within the recesses of the barn no night sight mattered at all. Our world was black.

His preference for the barn suggested that it was not the first time he had fought for his life in darkness. But in the battles of his guerrilla warfare he was festooned with full magazines for whatever weapon he used to spray his enemies. He could not use that technique. Past experience would not help to solve his ammunition problem. So we were equal. A sound had to be very promising indeed before either of us was likely to fire at it.

There were plenty of little sounds if one listened carefully – some made by rats, some by the settling of rotten wood and mortar after the plunging of the horses, some by Saint Sabas. It was difficult for either of us to move quietly. He was wearing riding boots; I, ordinary boots and leather gaiters. Three or four steps might be completely muffled by patches of chaff or dung dried to powder, but the next crackled on noisier debris.

I was sure that Saint Sabas had moved away from the far corner of the back wall where he had crouched to speak to me. He had crossed the barn to the front wall. An absolute silence from that direction – no rats, no movement – suggested that he was lying down in the angle of wall and floor close to the entrance, waiting for me to try to get out.

I decided on a booby trap to distract his attention. Close to my hand were the remains of a stable door, hanging from one hinge and swaying and creaking in the slightest breath of wind. I lifted a truss of hay and balanced it on the door. On the truss I laid my torch and covered it with more hay. I switched it on. No trace of light showed.

Then I moved on hands and knees to the angle of wall and floor on my side of the doorway. The wind or even a heavy footstep ought to bring the whole teetering pile down and give me a moment to leap out of the barn while Saint Sabas charged the light or shot at it.

There we lay, separated from each other by fifteen feet of lighter space into which neither dared venture. He was there, all right. I once heard him draw a deep breath. I was very tempted to risk a shot parallel to the wall and six inches above the floor. But if I missed or only wounded, exactly the same shot in reverse would get me.

I waited quarter of an hour for my delicately balanced bundle to collapse. It did not. No obliging rat. No puff of wind. Too ingenious. So I thought I might employ my time to better advantage. It would cost me a shot, but the shot might very well hit.

With infinite precautions I discarded my gaiters, took off my boots and stuffed them inside the top of my pullover with laces knotted behind my neck; I have never moved so slowly in my life. Then I started to circle the barn keeping close to the far wall so that I knew where I was. My plan was to crawl up behind Saint Sabas and shoot whether I could see him or not. He would assume that he was faintly visible, and his only possible move was to hurl himself away from the wall into deeper darkness. That gave me a split second to get through the door before he recovered from the shock.

The circling of the barn tried patience hard; but my long practice in moving imperceptibly counted. There were numerous small scraps of barbed wire and old iron about. Each foot had to go down slowly feeling for the floor. At last I struck the front wall, followed it towards the door and stopped a couple of yards short of the point where I believed Saint Sabas to be. I did not want to touch him. There was no telling what his exact position was. He might have heard me. Even if he hadn't, the instinct of the hunted could be strong enough to make him turn round to face the imagined danger.

Bent low and with my left hand on the ground I fired into the darkness ahead. Saint Sabas cursed and seemed to charge the spot where I had been but was not. I tip-toed in two strides round the doorpost and into the open.

So easy. So unhurried. And it was successful just because I had used my superiority in stalking, though not under the conditions I expected. I sat down and put on my boots. It was nearly as dark outside as in the barn. The wind had dropped. A soft, straight drizzle was falling. Low down on the horizon was the faint streak of the false dawn.

I lay down on the left of the door between the pile of rubble and the dung heap. He could never see me there until he stepped on me. If he tried to break out it was the end of him.

It was now my turn to wear down his nerves. He did not know whether I was inside or outside the barn; and he had to know, for time was against him. On the top of that, loss of blood from my first shot might be telling. All I had seen when he tried to ride me down was the edge of a stained cravat and his coat collar pinned up over it. The last shot, too, could have scored. His exclamation seemed to carry more than surprise, but whether pain or just anger I was not able to tell.

I intended him to waste himself by useless cunning and empty attacks until he lost patience. Meanwhile I waited, covering the door. Several times I heard him. Once he made a rush, but there was no shot. After that was silence. He was listening for me.

It was essential that he should go on thinking I was inside, so I cautiously heaved a clod of earth obliquely through the door. When it fell, it sounded exactly as if I had tripped over something soft. The result was a rustle of movement and an audible stumble. I could feel that his nerves were at last giving way. By this time there was a curious occult sympathy between us; I imagine it was the effect of intense concentration upon the other's mind. In another minute he would have charged out of the door, regardless of the consequences.

And then that blasted bundle of hay collapsed when it was no use to me. The torch rolled tinkling across the floor. It was still lit, of course. There was no immediate reaction from Saint Sabas. He was holding his breath and living only in his ears.

I never knew such a tiger of a man for swift decision. The lighted torch, falling without any sound or action to back it up, convinced him that I was not in the barn at all. If I was not, then it did not matter whether his figure was outlined for a second in the window. I might be watching it from the outside, but it was a hundred to one that I was watching the doorway. Perhaps that clod of earth clinched it. Whatever the object was, it had been thrown in through the door.

I heard him run across the barn and drop down to the ground through the window without any precautions at all. I ran on a parallel course along the outside wall, but arrived at the corner of the barn just too late. All I saw was a movement into the copse without any clear outline. I fired at it and he replied from the trees as I hurled myself into cover a few yards away from him.

This at last was the game as I wanted it to be played. I knew on which black square he was and the particular complex of shadows which held him. But the beech leaves underfoot were not packed and there were too many dead and crackling stems of some kind of umbellifera. To stalk him was not easy. It was impossible to move quietly – or quietly enough for ears trained by those hours of terror in the barn.

In a sense we were nearly always in sight of each other. But which shapeless spectre was man and which a bush or a tuft of coarse grass was hard to tell – unless, that is, it deliberately moved to draw a shot. Each knew that the other knew exactly what he had left in the magazine, and neither could be tempted by anything less than a certainty. Myself I would have considered a certainty any solid which still looked like part of a man at a range of a dozen feet.

He seldom used the ground for cover. His technique was to jump from tree to tree. As soon as I had appreciated that, I shepherded him towards the edge of the copse, which was at its narrowest behind the barn, hoping to force him out into the open, greyer than the wood though no longer moonlit.

But now, I think, he did take to the ground; and I could not turn his flank and keep him on the run without venturing into the open myself. That may have been just what he wanted me to do.

I had threatened him twice already with a noiseless approach over favourable ground; so, when silence had gone on long enough to alarm him, he retreated along the limit of the windbreak parallel to the barn. Still not a shot was fired. It was a savage hunting, all the more vile because of discipline. Neither would lose contact, but neither had any intention of being left with an empty gun. Two shots were not enough. It was so obvious that if one fired the other would reply at the flash, and then all must be staked on the last cartridge immediately. He must have longed, as I did, for both magazines to be exhausted and the way open for hands and the butt.

This was the only moment of the night which had any resemblance to a true duel. When there was movement it was quick and intense as lunge, parry, and ripost. Then came another interval while I tried to work round his flank.

Always I was the attacker, infiltrating behind him while he believed I was in front, and always he fell back from tree to tree to avoid the threat. Once either of us could have been killed. I had noiseless grass under my knees and I crept very close to a shadow which I had recognized as him. But where grass can grow there is some light from above. I remembered that just in time. When the shadow moved I was already poised to roll sideways into greater darkness. Even so no shot was fired. That was typical of the sudden engagements.

The pace was getting faster now. After all these weeks he was the hunted, and he knew it. He was driven back on the western side of the barn where the trees thinned out and the windbreak stood well back from the wall. I circled round outside him, trying to force him into the open or into a hopeless frontal attack. At last I pinned him on the edge of the open space, and little chance he had of moving to any other cover without offering a target. But the cover which he did have gave him a formidable position. He was cradled in the roots of a big beech. I doubted if I was looking at him. In any case there was no possibility of distinguishing the roundness of a body from the roundness of roots.

Conditions underfoot were satisfactory. The prevailing westerly winds sweeping round the corner of the barn had cleared away all leaves and debris. I cautiously disengaged and crawled back through the darkness of the copse parallel to the northern wall. When I was out of all possible sight I crossed the open strip to the wall itself, and began to work my way back along it towards the corner. There I was behind his position. It would be a longish shot – for that light – across the bare ground, but I reckoned I should have time to aim carefully.

Hugging the wall I peered round the northwest corner of the barn. I could not see him. I came to the conclusion that he must be standing up against the trunk of the tree.

He fired. The shot struck me full in the forehead. I was sure of that, yet the body refused to believe that it was dead. It scuttled away like a rat, back along the wall, and staggered into the safety of the trees. I think it even turned and twisted among them to throw off pursuit. It dropped behind some low, black thing, while the person carried in this automaton of terrified muscles put his hand to his forehead and collapsed.

I have the impression that my unconsciousness was not total; if it was, then there is some primitive saviour in the damaged animal watching on its behalf until the higher nervous centres regain control. Something must have been listening, for I knew that Saint Sabas had not followed me. That something, when I was capable of checking intuition, was right. There was no sound at all of riding boots shuffling lightly over leaves.

I raised my face just off the ground and took my hand away from my forehead. Immediately blood poured over my eyelids. Very delicately and still wondering, I dabbled in the mess. There was no hole in the skull.

Then what had happened? It seemed likely that I had forgotten dawn and misjudged the light. Saint Sabas, taking an occasional look behind him, had seen my head peering round the corner of the barn with insolent over-confidence against the streak of eastern sky. He had missed – but either the bullet ricocheting off the wall or a chunk of stone dislodged by it had ploughed across my forehead. I tried to get the flap of scalp back into position and bandage it with a handkerchief. I could not lift my hands behind my head to tie a knot. Again I fainted.

When I drifted back to consciousness the light was growing grey – still a dark grey, but where there were trees one behind another I could distinguish them all as separate. I was lying behind a fallen branch and easily to be seen if Saint Sabas looked for me. I could not understand why he was not on me already. He need not even use his last shot. A boot would do.

It was an effort to remember that he was human, that he had no power to follow scent or see in the dark. Of course his right game was to wait another ten minutes for a little more light and crouch over the blood trail which would lead him to me.

I remembered beasts from my shooting days before the war which I never found. Did they die or did they recover? They had a better chance of escaping than I. Often the loose skin, stretched by running, no longer corresponded with the hole in the flesh, and the blood trail petered out. Then the brown eyes, dull with pain and fear, must often have watched me pass the cover – likely as not another fallen branch – and go ignorantly away.

The light grew. Saint Sabas could see the blood now whenever he chose to look. There must be little pools of it, not just traces on grass and leaf. A scalp wound, when fresh, is the messiest of all.

At last I heard him. He was still opposite the western side of the barn and trying to choke down a fit of coughing – which, earlier, would have killed him. The effort he made reminded me that in his eyes I was still dangerous.

I had forgotten that he too was wounded, once if not twice. That was the likeliest reason why he had not charged out after me when I was hit; he was thankful for a rest. Whether dying or not, at any rate I was out of action. He could be sure that this time I was not bluffing. With a bit of luck I might be blind. But meanwhile I still had two rounds in the magazine.

He was right. I was not harmless at all, and if I could lie up safely a little longer I might still have a last spring in me. Through all these minutes of half conscious self-pity I had been identifying myself with some harmless creature dying defenceless in the forest. But it was I who was the wounded tiger, not he. I raised my head for the first time and looked round. My fallen branch gave no cover for even half light, and patches of blood must point straight at it.

Was it possible to change position? If I were going to try, I must begin at once. I could not. The thought of any physical action was so repugnant that I welcomed excuses. I should faint in the open. I should leave such a trail that it was futile to hide myself. In imagination I could see him bobbing intently from tree to tree until he reached ... but until he reached whatever I wanted him to reach, of course!

It was a grim and cruel thought from which to recover morale. Yet that was its effect. If I could find the strength to lay a blood trail which led past the barrel of the Mauser, I and my future were safe.

I looked round for some shelter, not too far away, into which I could reasonably have stumbled at the end of my first blind rush. There were two possibilities. One was a bit of broken wall near the edge of the windbreak; the other, a little hollow which might once have taken the overflow of the spring. Neither was any use for defence, but both had to be approached closely before St Sabas could see whether my body was lying on the ground.

To one or the other I had to make a followable trail. When

he came across the matted blood and leaves behind the branch where I had collapsed, it must be clear to him in what direction I had crawled on. Whether I chose wall or hollow, he would not walk straight up to it, but would try to work his way round and take a look from any convenient cover.

I could not distinguish clearly all the details of grey mass. I was looking, however, into a part of the copse to the right of the central clearing which I had reconnoitred carefully on my first arrival at the barn in some previous existence and into which I had dodged when escaping from Saint Sabas's mounted attack. So the blurred picture, though without detail, made sense.

The hollow was very simple to outflank, and if he were reasonably careful while engaged in stalking it I had no chance of ambushing him. The wall was more promising. There were two low bramble bushes on the edge of the windbreak which commanded it. The way to put a last shot into an old goat lying helpless behind the wall was to pass round the outside of the copse, re-enter it and look down on him between or over the brambles.

That was all right so far as it went. Yet the plan was no more than a sick man's dream unless I could find the strength to carry it out. I raised myself to hands and knees. They did not belong to me, but they worked.

I had to cover thirty flat and simple yards over a sparse carpet of last year's fallen leaves. I assured myself that it was easy, provided I took it slowly and remembered to collapse quietly. The handkerchief had adhered to my forehead. To pull it off was the hardest task. I was absurdly terrified of the result, and my hand twice refused to do it.

The final jerk overdid the job. When I started to crawl the blood trail was spectacular. I forced myself to remember that it was only a surface cut, that one could lose pints of blood and that all I had lost probably didn't add up to one. I tried to convince myself that this fast dripping had nothing to do with my weakness and that I was just suffering from concussion. That – a purely mental thing – ought to be under the control of the will, and it had to be if I wanted to live.

Half way to my destination I think I began to laugh a little, for I recall being shocked at such levity. What had amused me was the thought that all this was in vain. Savarin was a fighter, not a tracker. Would he ever notice blood on red-brown beech leaves? I swore at him and dripped on to a flat white stone. Then I found another and dripped on that.

I reached the tumbledown wall and dropped behind it. I had been right; the damp patch of shadow between the mossed stones and the bramble bushes was just the sort of refuge which a wounded animal would choose. Binding the flap of scalp back into position, I rested. My hands could now tie a knot of sorts, which gave me confidence. I suppose the effort had done me good – had held off the effect of shock perhaps. Shock seems to be a killer of birds and the smallest mammals and man, not of a large and angry beast.

It was time for the second move – the move which left no trail at all. The full twilight of dawn had come, but most of the barn was now between me and my enemy – if, that is, he were still behind it or on the western side of it. And if he wasn't, it was all up anyway.

I rose to my feet and staggered from tree to tree until I was out of that hated, loathsome windbreak and could drop on to the thyme-scented hill turf. The fold of ground along which I had attacked after leaving Nur Jehan was close and would do for my purpose. I squirmed into it, facing the bramble bushes so that I would not have to move again to fire. The grass hid me well enough so long as Saint Sabas did not look for me. Light suddenly grew very much better. I think I must have had a short period of unconsciousness.

The windbreak appeared surprisingly small. It seemed incredible that there had been room in it for so much juggling with the art of murder. But its darkness was understandable. That canopy of dripping leaves, now nearly green, was solid enough for some lush, wooded valley.

The dawn chorus of birds was of splendid volume and variety. I could hear nothing else. All depended on sight, yet I dared not raise my head for a level look at the copse. I had to content myself with a swift glance every few seconds, for it gave me an intolerable headache to keep my eyes strained upwards. Even so nothing was clear. I did not know that I had seen Saint Sabas until I noticed what I had taken to be a tree trunk glimpsed between branches was no longer there.

My plan then was working. If he had come from the fallen branch to the edge of the windbreak it could only mean that the blood trail was dictating his movements. I lay very still, for it was certain that he would take no risks.

He quietly emerged from the trees at the far corner and began to work his way towards me. He was very tired and a little unsteady on his feet. His left arm was tucked into his coat; the sleeve was darker than the rest of the cloth. That was my shot when escaping from the barn, and that was why he had preferred to fight on his feet rather than his stomach. I like to think – but it may be hypocrisy – that I felt a stirring of pity for him, which fear all night had prevented.

It was very quickly extinguished. He began the stalk of the bramble bushes. His body, slanting forward, followed the black Colt in his right hand. He was intent as any beast of prey nosing inch by inch into the wind. Once he stopped and looked straight over me across the colourless turf. It was a possible chance, but I was in no state for snapshooting. He would have seen me as I raised head and shoulders to fire, and jumped into the trees. I needed a lot of time to aim; even an unhurried shot when he reached the bushes might be beyond me. The range was all of thirty-five yards.

He arrived at his objective and crouched behind the brambles. Evidently he did not like the prospect of putting his head over the top to see what was between them and the wall. He tried to find a gap, but there wasn't one and the undergrowth crackled as he pressed against it. I heard him over the singing of the birds. He realized that he was going about it the wrong way and that it was much safer to stand up and look quickly into the recess.

It was now or never. I rested my elbows squarely, holding the wrist of my right hand with my left. The barrel of the Mauser was reasonably steady, but blood dripped over my eyes at the critical moment. I forced myself not to hurry the shot, to take all the time in the world, to remember that it did not matter if he looked round and saw me.

He discovered that there was nothing behind the wall, no man dying or still dangerous. He stood up to his full height with a movement of impatience, turned and caught sight of that deadly little triangle on the ground formed by my head and forearms.

With the speed which was characteristic of him he took his only chance and fired. I paid no attention. I knew that only an aimed shot could hit at that range – or perhaps I was concentrating so desperately that I could not be distracted. I squeezed the trigger.

It was low for the heart, but it would do. Saint Sabas spun with the shot, holding his side. I never expected him to move any more after such a raking internal wound. It was not enough to stop a beast, but a man, yes. Men knew what had happened to them.

But he came on. Staggering on feet which would hardly carry him he came on, with nothing but bare hands. It was automatic, a last flare of his insanity of revenge. I was at the end of my resistance. Whenever I covered him the barrel of the Mauser sagged. He must have travelled five hideous, agonizing paces before I got him in the sights, more by accident than anything else, and this time heard the bullet strike. I had hit him high up on the thigh and smashed the bone. Poor devil. Magnificent fighter. He lay down rather than dropped, and put his head in his hands.

For me the night returned. I was hunting through dark woods, trying to find Benita or sometimes hunting Benita herself with an appalling sense of guilt which I tried to persuade myself I had no need to feel. There were policemen in Gestapo uniforms though I knew they were British, and the forest extended over the whole sphere of the world so that there was never any way out of it and never any more light to be. It was wrong and worrying when at last there was a great deal of sunlit grass beyond my toes. I opened my eyes still further. I was lying on my back, and there was a blue-peaked cap bending over me and taking up too much of the glorious relieving sky. I twitched my hand to push it away.

'Feeling better, Mr Dennim?'

This time I really lifted a hand. My head was beautifully bandaged. I was covered with a blanket. The policeman supported my shoulders and offered me hot, sweet tea. It worked like alcohol.

'A flesh wound only, isn't it?' I asked.

'Well, yes – if that's what you call "only".'

'He is dead?'

'He's in a bad way. We're waiting for the ambulance. Meanwhile would you care to tell us what happened?'

An inspector apeared from behind me, cleared his throat and slightly shook his head. He looked sympathetic, but extremely neutral. I vaguely remembered that there was some rule about not questioning persons to be charged with a crime until they were in a fit state to be cautioned.

'What brought you here?' I asked.

'That stallion of yours rampaging down the Tewkesbury road. Traffic police picked him up together with a mare. Both of them were saddled so it looked as if there had been an accident. They got one of the hunt whips out of bed to catch the horses, and he did some telephoning and found out who they belonged to. An aunt of yours said there was a Miss Gillon staying at Stow-on-the-Wold who would probably know where you were, and she did.'

'What did you tell Miss Gillon?'

'We couldn't tell her anything except that you might have had a fall. Your aunt was very insistent that Miss Gillon should stay where she was instead of getting lost herself, so that she could guide an admiral somebody up to the barn. A lot of sense the lady has, though I wouldn't say her telephone manner was what I'd call good.'

'How long have you been here?'

'About half an hour. It all took time.'

I longed for the admiral and Georgina, but the car which came slowly bumping over the turf was not his. The hill gave an impression of early morning before a race meeting. There were little groups of people drifting up from the villages and looking for places with a good view from which they would not be ordered back by the police.

The car was allowed to drive right up to us. Out of it jumped Sir Thomas Pamellor, more shrimp-like than ever – for he was unbrushed, unshaven and bristling with anxiety and importance. He didn't recognize me, didn't even look. I was just a vulgar and unpleasant casualty.

'I say, Callender, what's all this?' he asked.

'We are a little doubtful, Sir Thomas,' the inspector answered. 'On the face of it, there seems to have been a quarrel.'

'What? Teddy boys at it again? But what's it got to do with my guest never coming home? He said he might be late, so I wasn't bothering till I heard the mare had been picked up on the Tewkesbury road. I hope they haven't molested him in any way. Such a shocking example for a distinguished Frenchman!'

'What is his name, sir?'

'The Vicomte de Saint Sabas. And very pro-British, Callender! His mother's family ... God bless my soul, what was their name? Two little "f"s. Not fforde, not ffolliot, not ffoulkes. Anyway his grandfather owned a lot of land in Northamptonshire. Oh, a very useful friend of this country! At heart he is just as English as I am French. Now, if only there were a few more people like us ...'

'Would that be him, sir?'

I felt able to sit up and look round. A little way out from the edge of the copse, where he had fallen, two constables and a doctor were bending over him. Sir Thomas bustled across and cried out:

'Saint Sabas! Good God!'

The man was unkillable. He appeared to murmur something, for I could see Sir Thomas listening. He came bounding back.

'Look here, inspector, what has been going on? I am a magistrate and I have a right to be told.'

'We don't know, sir. A neighbour of yours, Admiral Cunobel, called up headquarters as soon as he heard about the Arab horse and told them that Mr Dennim was in danger of his life. But the Vee ... the, er ... your friend cannot explain yet.'

'In danger of his life? From Saint Sabas? Quite impossible, Callender!' Sir Thomas exploded. 'I knew the Vicomte well before the war. Used to shoot with him. I don't say he wouldn't engage in an affair of honour. I'm French enough myself to understand that a quiet meeting is preferable to all that nasty English publicity of a libel action. But where are the seconds? We should find them here. To my mind this is a perfectly plain case of attempted murder, and you should charge this fellow at once. I know him. Lunched with me! I had a very unfavourable impression. An international adventurer, I understand. The French thought somebody wanted to blow him up. I should advise you to let Scotland Yard know immediately.'

He turned on me, as if I were unfortunate enough to be under his command.

'What have *you* got to say for yourself, Dennim?'

'Nothing,' I answered.

'But you – you may have killed him.'

I said I thought it very likely.

'This was a – a duel, what?'

'You could call it that.'

'What are you?' he blustered. 'I don't believe you're English at all.'

'More, sir, at any rate than I was yesterday.'

He stared at me, outraged.

'Caution him and take a statement, inspector!'

'I think we had better be patient a little longer, Sir Thomas,' said Inspector Callender imperturbably.

I lay back, for I had used up too much energy answering insolence with insolence. I had an uneasy feeling that when Saint Sabas prophesied in the inn garden that I should be tried for my life, he was probably right. The police were very kind and – which surprised me – gentle. But I was too conscious of their passionless faces; I mean, that closed expression which assumes the worst of human nature while assuring you that everything is for the best, that juries are sensible and warders understanding and cells very comfortable and that you may pin up a picture of your wife after the first six months. It's what we pay 'em for, Jim Melton said.

Another car was in sight, leaping over the rutted track without any regard at all for the springs. I had no doubt that the admiral was in it. He had first made a name for himself in command of a destroyer at the Battle of Jutland, and attacked an empty road in the same spirit. I was so glad to see him that I nearly passed out again.

He dashed out of the car, making a commanding gesture to the passengers in the back that they were to stay where they were.

'Great Blood and Bones, boy! Not got you, has he?'

I told him I was all right except for a cut across the scalp, and begged him to do any explaining he could.

'Ah, Cunobel!' Sir Thomas interrupted. 'Glad you're here! You'll be a great help to me. A guest of mine, the Vicomte de St Sabas, has been assassinated.'

'Saint Sabas? Saint Sabas? I used to know his mother very well.'

The admiral looked questioningly at me, and I nodded.

'I'm afraid this fellow Dennim has taken in the pair of us completely,' Sir Thomas went on. 'As it is, I'm having trouble with the police. I insist on him being cautioned and charged.'

'Charge him? Charge my aunt!' Cunobel roared. '*Bougrez* off, Pamellor! *Bougrez* off, as they say in French! If you want someone to listen to you, you bloody fool, go and send a signal to the cabinet!'

He knelt down beside me and eased me back on to the police pillow with fatherly tenderness.

'I've got Georgina and the Gillon girl in the car. I told 'em they had to wait till I found out how the land lay. His aunt,' he explained to the inspector, 'the only close relative. You've had a talk with her on the telephone already, eh? She's always right, but it takes plain chaps like you and me time to recover, eh? Shall I let them loose, Charles?'

I said doubtfully that I was not a pretty sight. I did not want Benita dragged into this. But he pulled the blanket up to my chin and beckoned to the car.

Benita ran ahead. She gave no other sign of anxiety. She played the well-brought-up Englishwoman, determined to keep a strange world out of our private lives. I had not seen her in the part before, and it disturbed me that her quick, vivid face should be so deliberately empty.

'That blasted horse!' she said.

It took me an appreciable second to remember that she knew nothing. I couldn't start explaining. I just assured her that a couple of days in hospital were all I needed, and asked after Nur Jehan.

'Daddy is down at the hunt stables,' she answered venomously, 'holding his hand after his night out.'

Concentrating on me, she had not taken in the scene at all. She turned pale as she saw the group on the edge of the copse, the serious faces, the blood-stained swabs on the ground. A police sergeant passed carrying by their barrels, wrapped in his handkerchief, the Colt and the Mauser. She understood too much all at once, and the implications of it overwhelmed control.

'So you *were* expecting someone!'

She burst into passionate tears. Not hysteria. Just the intolerable grief of youth escaping from its education.

Georgina held her.

'I can take it you are not seriously hurt, Charles?' she asked.

'No, dear Georgi.'

'You seem to have been very lucky. Benita, there is no reason to carry on like an Italian whose second cousin has just died of old age.'

'He was so alone,' Benita sobbed. 'Always alone.'

'My darling, I had to be,' I answered. 'But if it weren't for you I should be dead.'

Georgina realized that she had no more need to reproach me for stubbornness towards Benita. But she was puzzled. She thought that Benita had in some way averted an attack on me. I tried to explain what I meant: that after surrender to love and the country of one's love one no longer makes the lonely, empty gestures of a man whose only home is in his pride.

'Engaged to Benita!' the admiral exclaimed. 'Couldn't be better! I never could understand why you carried on as if you wouldn't see eighty again. Why, when I was in my forties ...'

'Yes, Peregrine?' said my aunt.

'Damn it, Georgi, I was in Budapest on the Danube Commission! Look here, inspector, be a good fellow and keep this under your hat! Miss Gillon is just Nur Jehan's sister, eh? I mean, it's her father's stallion, and that's the only reason why she is here. You never heard of romance, eh? We don't want the news hawks bothering them on that one. I give you my word the boy won't go to trial. But he's bound to have an awkward week or two.'

The inspector had fallen completely under Cunobel's charm. He nodded, but remained with pencil poised over his notebook. 'Miss Gillon did not know the – the other gentleman?' he asked.

'Miss Gillon, inspector,' said Aunt Georgina, 'was quite unaware that my nephew was sacrificing himself to catch a murderer. Even I myself was partly deceived. Peregrine, I shall speak to you afterwards. There is no doubt in my mind that you knew a great deal more than you were telling me, and I can only hope that at your club or possibly your wine merchant's –' we were given to understand that she remembered the Madeira and had put two and two together '– you have made the acquaintance of some other confirmed bachelor who is a person of authority in the Home Office.'

'Yes, Georgi. I know the Assistant Commissioner of Special Branch. But I'm afraid he's not a bachelor. Is he a bachelor, inspector?'

'I could not say, sir,' said the inspector stolidly – he wanted to smile, but he was not risking an engagement with Georgina. 'Any statement which you wish to make should be given in the first place to Gloucester police.'

Statements. Mr Dennim told me this. Mr Dennim told me that. Well, no doubt in weeks or months they would dig up some direct evidence which Counsel for the prosecution could not so easily ignore.

The ambulance which arrived and pulled alongside the inspector depressed me even more. I should have been glad enough to see it two hours earlier; but now it emphasized the immediacy of the parting from Benita and too sudden a plunge from the savagery of the night into inhuman tranquillity. What had this white, impersonal machine for the mending of bodies to do with a darkness which was more real than the warmth of the sun on my face? I spoke and lived in the present, but the optic nerves were still trying to distinguish my enemy from trees.

'Almighty Wings, you aren't going to bung 'em both in together, are you?' Cunobel protested.

I looked to my left. Saint Sabas, carried on a stretcher, was about to pass behind me.

'Put me down beside that gentleman,' he said.

It was a surprisingly clear and definite whisper. The two bearers hesitated. I raised myself on my elbows and looked at him. He was entirely covered by blankets. His once dark face was icy white. The lobe of his left ear was shot away but had stopped bleeding. They had not bothered with that at all in the urgency of his other wounds. He tried to smile.

'Please put him down,' I asked.

It never occurred to me to say anything else. That we should speak seemed so natural. What we had shared we had shared.

'Graf von Dennim, I have lain there thinking about you. I wanted to say that I believe you. I think I did believe you even at the inn. I have had enough to do with officers of the – of the service which duty compelled you to join. They are not men of courage.

'Apology is a meaningless word for us. And forgiveness, perhaps. But I wish to ask you a question. May I?'

'Of course.'

'She only walked? She was quite dead?'

'She was already dead, Saint Sabas.'

'Thank you,' he gasped. 'You could not know who or what she was. I am proud that when she had nothing more to give she could still help. And now – you said something which made me believe you had respect for my name.'

'I do.'

With a last hoarse whispering from his indomitable energy he broke into rapid German. He must have spoken it perfectly when he was in a state to remember words.

'Then I will dare to appeal to you. I do not want to be saved. Your first shot went through me. The kidney, I think. But the damned doctors might patch me up for the scaffold yet. Your second cut the femoral artery. I put on a tourniquet. I thought I might still crawl. Thank God I could not! So at last there was nothing left to do but think.

'They have put on their own tourniquet. Under the blanket I am about to undo it. The result will be obvious if I am lifted off the ground. Please, if you can, keep me with you a moment.'

Sir Thomas Pamellor was busy giving orders to which no one paid any attention. The inspector, momentarily confused by him, could not intervene effectively. But the evidence of collusion between Saint Sabas and myself was suspicious. So was the interest on the faces of the admiral and Georgina.

'Were you able to follow what was being said, sir?' the inspector asked.

'Never could understand German!' Cunobel lied. 'Impossible language!'

'I am so sorry. Nor do I,' said Georgina.

'I'm not going to stand for it, inspector!' Sir Thomas exclaimed. 'This is a clear case of attempted murder. I know very well what the Vicomte is going to say. It's what I'd do myself. A great, Christian gentleman ...'

'I am neither,' Saint Sabas murmured. 'Bend down, inspector! Take my statement and do not interrupt! I, Raoul Philippe Humphrey, Vicomte de Saint Sabas, of Saint Sabas in the Department of Maine et Loire, solemnly declare that I endeavoured to kill – to assassinate this gentleman and that he has killed me in self-defence. The motive remains between him and myself. If ever he can bring himself to make it public, he will only do honour to his own name and will give such little as he can to mine.

'I confess that in Western Germany I killed three war criminals named Gustav Sporn, Walter Dickfuss and Hans Weber. I do not regret it. I regret only that I should have wasted so much of my life upon so worthless a compulsion.

'I confess, too, with bitter shame and sorrow, that it was I who sent the bomb which killed a postman serving Charles Dennim's house, and I desire that the welfare of the man's family shall be a first charge upon my estate. If brought to trial,

I should plead insanity. Death is a very kind deliverance, for me as for my dear wife.'

He freed his left hand from the blanket and held it out to Sir Thomas Pamellor.

'Will you hold my hand a minute – for old friendship?'

'You – you – you murdered a postman!' Pamellor stammered.

The hand fell to the ground, so limp that it made an audible little thud.

'No one,' Saint Sabas muttered. 'No one knows enough. Only Dennim.'

'I have always understood, Savarin,' I answered.

He drew out his right hand, bright red and dripping, and laid it on the turf between us with the last of his strength. For the few seconds which were left, it was I who held it between my own.